MY
VILLAGE
IN THE
VALLEY

These stories are dedicated to all the friends in our village who made us so welcome when we moved from a city with a population of 67,000 to a village with a population of 300. You are not the people in these stories, my friends, and neither is 'The Village in the Valley' our village, but by absorbing us so effortlessly into community life you freed my imagination to write these stories.

Thank you.

Crumps Barn Studio
Crumps Barn, Syde, Cheltenham GL53 9PN
www.crumpsbarnstudio.co.uk

Cover design by Lorna Gray © Crumps Barn Studio

Printed in Gloucestershire on FSC certified paper by Severn, a carbon neutral company

ISBN 978-1-915067-00-5

MICHAEL BARTLETT

MY VILLAGE IN THE VALLEY

In the country, nothing
is ever simple...

Crumps Barn Studio

There are two contrary impulses which govern this man's brain – the one sane, and the other eccentric. They alternate at regular intervals.

Franz Schubert

A note from the author:

In these stories …
The village is fictional …
The people are fictional …
The events depicted … are semi-fictional …
The emotions and feelings are true.

However, I suspect that anyone who has ever lived in a village will find some of this familiar. Real life is always more outrageous than *The Archers*.

THERE'S NO
POINT SITTING
ON AN ACORN

It wasn't just the refusal of the County Highways Department to consider traffic calming measures in our village, it was their statement that not enough people had been killed that so enraged our Parish Council chairman, Marjorie Fawcett.

"I can hardly believe this," she told a particularly stormy meeting of the Council, "but they say we don't just need recorded deaths, they have to have happened at the same place. Apparently one at the western edge of the village and two at the eastern end wouldn't count."

My Village in the Valley, like many other rural villages across the country, has long suffered from speeding traffic and inconsiderate drivers. This response from County Highways was the final blow in an on-going campaign to try and deal with the problem. At every Parish Council meeting since time immemorial there was a report of yet another incident, a crash here, a near miss there and occasionally a cat, dog or chicken run over, but nothing ever got done. The trouble was that highways are outside the jurisdiction of the Parish Council. Highways are a County Council responsibility and our County Town is a long way off.

One particularly horrendous period saw a lorry in the river, an allotment shed wrapped round the screen of a Range Rover and a telegraph pole converted from the vertical to the horizontal. After that, the Parish Council applied to have 'traffic calming measures' installed. Anything that forced the traffic to slow down would do, flashing speed signs, chicanes at each end of the village, a real speed camera, whatever would be most effective. One Councillor was in favour of land mines but as it was generally agreed that the people in the County Highways Department, like all public officials, were unlikely to have a sense of humour, that suggestion was not passed on.

Following the application, there was no response for six months in spite of constant reminders from the Parish Clerk. Eventually a letter was sent to the Chief Executive of the County Council demanding a reply. The response from County Highways was that they'd never received such a request.

The letters and emails were produced, copied and sent to them again. Another two months went by and eventually the answer came back that nothing could be done. The letter said that the expense of traffic calming measures was not justified as not enough people had been killed in the village. When the Clerk enquired how many bodies they needed before they would act, she was told – verbally – three at the same place. This was the comment that so enraged Marjorie Fawcett.

The Parish Council was unimpressed, but there was nothing more they could do. They'd made a request, it had been refused and there were no grounds for an appeal. Not officially that is, but some of us have little patience with bureaucratic stupidity so we decided to kick some ideas around between ourselves.

My Village in the Valley is a quiet unassuming place where, on the whole, very little happens, the sort of place social historians refer to as 'a real community'. My neighbours are a broad mix. Some, like me, were born in the village. Some, unlike me, have families which go back generations here. Some are incomers, from elsewhere in the county or from further afield, but most have been absorbed into village life and we don't take kindly to outsiders telling us what to do.

The real problem is that our main street is quite narrow. Also, at the western end of the street there's an awkward junction where the road splits sharply into a V, left and right, with the church in the island in the middle. At the other end of the street there's a tight right-hand turn by the allotments where the road crosses the river on a stone bridge only just wide enough to take a lorry.

Unfortunately, our village lies on a convenient rat-run, a shortcut for traffic from our local market town to connect with the main north/south road that runs through the county.

There is of course a 30 mile an hour speed limit with signs at each end of the village, but these are constantly ignored and not just ignored but treated with contempt. Speeds of 40 are common and 50 mph or more is not unusual, and there are frequent crashes on the bridge where someone travelling too fast insists on a right of way.

Sadly, these speeding drivers rarely hit each other – if they did the problem might be self-solving – instead they either hit the bridge, which causes a lot of damage to the parapet, or they end up in the allotments which means the carrots and cauliflowers suffer.

There was a strong feeling in the village that something had to be done. The official approach having failed, we were left with the unofficial option so a few of us gathered together one evening in The Spy to talk it through.

The proper name of our village pub, the one listed on the landlord's licence, is *The One-Armed Spyglass,* an obscure name to many people until they realise that the reference is to Nelson who had connections with this county. In fact, Nelson never came near our village and we're a long way from the sea, but the naming of English pubs has always defied logic.

When we were all settled and the first round bought, Rupert opened the discussion by putting two postcards down on the table. Rupert's family have farmed in this area for generations. Rupert himself was the cowman for one of the local landowners until supermarket greed forced the dairy herd to be sold so Rupert now runs a small building firm in the nearby market town.

Both postcards were faded sepia photographs of the village street in 1895. Nothing much has changed, except the old school has long since been converted into a private house. The photos clearly show the narrowness of the street, the sharp curve onto the bridge at the eastern end and the V-junction at the western end. On one side of the street is a line of old farm workers cottages, all long since sold off and modernised inside. The shop, nestling among the cottages, stands facing the pub and village car park, a space where dray horses were once tethered while the barrels were unloaded.

"The problem is," said Rupert, "that nothing's really changed since 1895 except the size and the volume of the traffic."

"Well, there's not much chance of road widening," said Sylvia, "Most of those cottages are Grade 2 listed. I had enough trouble getting permission to put in double glazing."

Bill nodded. "And the other side you've got the pub—"

"—Which is also Grade 2."

"True, but in any case, it stands on the riverbank. so there's no room anyway."

Nigel made the obvious point that the narrow bridge was the bottleneck.

"Just as well," said Harry, "any wider and they'd drive even faster."

"Look, let's cut to the chase," said Jessica in her usual no-nonsense way. "There's no point in sitting on an acorn."

Jessica is one of our more recent arrivals in the village. She used to be a television producer and is now a freelance theatre director. A determined lady who hadn't yet quite adjusted to the rhythm of life here.

We all looked at her blankly and she sighed, exasperated as always by people not understanding her references.

"It's a saying," she explained. "There are three ways you can get to the top of a tree. You can make friends with a bird who will carry you up, you can climb it, or you can sit on an acorn and wait for it to grow."

"Phoebe Jones has a cockatoo," offered Dan, the landlord of The Spy, from his place behind the bar.

"What we need is direct action," said Jessica, "there's no point in going on about what we can't do. Let's try and sort out what we can do."

"Fair point," said Harry, "so what options do we have?"

"Well, if all official channels are closed to us," said Sylvia, "we have to look at the unofficial ones."

There was a short silence then Bill said, "Well, I do have one idea."

Bill is ex-army, Royal Engineers, to be exact. He took early retirement and became a security consultant, so he believes in going for the jugular.

"Let's get rid of the bridge," he said, "turn the river crossing into a ford. That would slow the traffic down."

He was clearly longing to be asked to assemble a demolition squad and blow the whole structure sky-high but the general feeling was that this was too dramatic and in any case, as Nigel, our retired solicitor, pointed out, legal removal of the bridge would still require the permission of the County Highways Department since the bridge was part of the public road.

Jessica was in favour of hiring a private detective to investigate the senior officials at County Highways to see if we could dig up any dirt to blackmail them with. Harry suggested yellow lines but was immediately shouted down. First they were unsightly, second they only prevented parking, not speeding, and thirdly they would still require permission from Highways.

Jessica made the point that blackmail didn't require anyone's permission, just determination and a strong nerve.

Sylvia wondered if it would be worthwhile going over the heads of the officials at County Highways and appealing direct to a government minister to obtain traffic calming measures but, after some discussion it was decided that this plan would cost too much in back-handers, and in any case wouldn't carry any guarantee of success.

Jessica said that if we wouldn't consider blackmailing County Highways, then why not purchase a few dead bodies, position them in strategic positions, take photos and bribe one of the local doctors to certify them as traffic accidents. We considered this briefly in the time it took Harry to get another round in, but finally rejected it as being too complicated to set up and could backfire on us.

It was felt that Jessica was letting her artistic background get the better of her, but she pointed out that we wouldn't even need real bodies. She knew enough out-of-work actors who would happily lie down in the road for a few quid in cash while we took photos of them.

Sylvia suggested we ask the police to mount more regular speed checks within the village. In the past whenever they did that they caught a lot of people but they didn't come often enough.

Dan came out from behind the bar to collect our empties and he joined in.

"Forget the police," he said, "they don't have time for speed checks. Tom was telling me the other night …"

"Who?" asked Jessica.

""Tom Riley," said Rupert. "He's our local policeman. What they call the local beat manager. He's a great guy."

"Yes," said Dan, "but he's a great guy with too much to do. Until last month he had four villages to look after. Now he has eight and they've taken his Community Support Officer away so now he's on his own."

"Why've they done that?" asked Jessica.

"To save money," said Dan. "Someone's got to

pay for that Police and Crime Commissioner bloke that no-one wanted or voted for."

There was a short silence as we contemplated the scale of the problem we faced.

We were on the third round when inspiration finally struck. We had just, rather reluctantly it's true, rejected Jessica's latest suggestion that she should hire a camera crew, film the worst of the speeders and post the videos on YouTube with scathing comments about their driving, when Harry cut the Gordian knot. He drained his glass, put it down on the table with a thump and said that we were getting away from the main point. We weren't particularly interested in catching the speeders, what we wanted was to stop them speeding in the first place.

We all nodded wisely and Harry went on to point out that the only time you could be sure of traffic going slowly along the village street was when a lorry was parked delivering something.

"Good point," said Bill. "Perhaps we could organise a rota of deliveries so there's always a lorry parked somewhere."

"No, said Rupert; "there's an easier solution. If we can rustle up a couple of old tractors, or vans and such and park them in the street, then we'd effectively create our own chicane."

"They'd still have to be licensed," said Nigel, "and

have a current MOT or they'd be illegal and could be removed."

"Not a problem," said Rupert, "I can certainly provide one van and I'm sure we can get others."

Sylvia said she would speak to Roger Fraser who farmed the land at the western end of the village. She was pretty sure he'd lend us a tractor on rotation. Dan said we could borrow his old Land Rover for some of the time and Bill said we could use his wife's Volvo. Typical Bill.

And so it was decided. Although this was private enterprise, so to speak, we thought it only courteous to let Marjorie Fawcett, as Parish Council chairman, know what we were doing. Harry agreed to talk her and later told us she could hardly keep the grin off her face and immediately offered her Morris Traveller Estate as part of the team.

That gave us five vehicles to play with and it soon became apparent that we'd need all of them.

The following Monday we started with Rupert's van and Roger's tractor which we moved into strategic positions, one of each side of the road, spaced just far enough apart for the emergency services to get through but close enough to force vehicles to slow down. This worked reasonably well for a few days, but then Jessica spotted another problem.

"The traffic's going slower," she said, "but we're

not really causing the drivers any inconvenience."

"Well, we can't completely block the traffic on a public highway," said Sylvia, "anyway slowing them down was the whole idea."

"No, Jessica's got a point," said Bill, "We're winning the battle but not the war. We can't keep these vehicles on the street indefinitely. We need a long-term solution."

"Like proper traffic calming measures," said Nigel.

"Which County Highways have already said no to," said Sylvia.

"Then we'll have to make them change their minds," said Bill.

Once again it was Harry who finally cracked it. As a retired merchant banker, a devious mind presumably goes with the job. His scheme, like most good schemes, was simple. It took us ten days or so to get it all organised but once it was launched, the result was immediate.

Using the various vehicles at our disposal in rotation, we parked two on one side of the road and one between them on the other. This meant that traffic passing along the street had to zig-zag between them and if something was coming the other way, one set had to stop to let them through. That was pretty good, but Harry's plan was even more cunning. Two of the vehicles, one on each side of the road, were parked close enough together so that a lorry or a large vehicle could not actually get through. There was nothing illegal in this, there were no parking restrictions in the street, but it was not something people would normally do.

However, the result was that every time a large vehicle couldn't get through it had to stop. The driver then hooted, of course, and after a moment someone would appear, smile sweetly, get into one of the offending cars and move it a few yards so the vehicle could get through. Once it had gone, the car would be moved back to a similar position until the next big vehicle appeared.

The really cunning parts of Harry's plan were that we had a rota of villagers with keys to the vehicles standing by so that although a delay and aggravation was caused, it never lasted very long. The second part was that each day the three stationary vehicles were left in different places along the street so there was no justification for them being described as 'abandoned' and forcibly removed.

Complaints from motorists and particularly haulage and bus companies poured in to the police and to the County Council but there was nothing illegal about our actions so there was nothing they could do.

The County Council and the Highways

Department knew exactly what we were doing and why of course. Apart from anything else the final stage of Harry's plan was a concentrated spate of letters and calls from people in the village and around the area, pointing out how much better and safer life was when the traffic was forced to go slower. The local and regional press were inundated with letters supporting slower traffic, many of them accompanied by pictures of dead cats and dogs which, it was alleged, had been killed by thoughtless (and illegal) speeding.

Personally, I am not sure we had ever had that many cats and dogs in the village but as we all know, a journalist never lets the truth get in the way of a good story.

It took three months but finally the County Highways Department gave in and we were promised chicanes at each end of the village street. Sylvia won the sweepstake with her two and half months estimate. Harry was over optimistic – he thought they'd cave in within a month. Nigel was way out with his six months guess. We did sustain a couple of casualties. Rupert's van had its back bumper redesigned and Marjorie Fawcett's Morris Traveller Estate lost its wing mirror and acquired a deep scratch down one side thanks to an impatient van driver.

A small price to pay really. In due course the chicanes were installed, the various vehicles went back to their owners and the village rota of standby drivers was disbanded. Then a few weeks later we held a benefit Bingo night in the village hall and raised enough money to get Marjorie's car repaired. A triumph of people power over bureaucracy.

THE LAST CHARGE
OF THE TRICYCLE

My Village in the Valley is never short of imaginative ideas. For example, our annual fête, or carnival as we prefer to call it, is always an extremely ambitious event although it usually ends up as a triumph of optimism over experience. The villagers come along in force, not just local people either, visitors come from far and wide though there is a strong suspicion that the main attraction is to see yet another disaster unfold. If so, they are seldom disappointed.

The year that Boudicca met the Romans in pitch battle is a case in point. On this occasion the person responsible for turning mayhem into farce was Newton Flotman.

Newton lived with his mother, Mabel, in one of the old farm cottages on the far side of the bridge. Mabel was a familiar sight to locals and visitors alike as she pedalled through the village on her vintage tricycle, towing a soap box behind her for the shopping, her cape streaming out behind her like a galleon under full sail. Although she wasn't exactly an educated woman, she was a fervent admirer of the great 17th century scientist, after whom she had christened her only son. Some of the older villagers maintained she was particular interested in the way Isaac Newton pursued the alchemy idea of turning base metals into gold and there were dark mutterings about what she got up to in her garden shed.

Be that as it may, Newton Flotman had never liked his name, said it made him sound like a small village on a main road somewhere, so he raised no objections when people started calling him Newt instead. However, as he got older people started linking him to the expression about newts which implied they were in a constant state of inebriation, and as Newt was a teetotaller this was more upsetting than being linked with a main road conurbation and he let it be known that he was not happy.

But Newt he was and Newt he stayed until the night of the great supermarket debate.

It was way, way back, when the concept of large retail parks on the edge of towns was still a novel idea, that Briscoe's, the supermarket chain, tried to buy a four acre site on the edge of our village to build, as they put it, "an out of town shopping experience". The village was outraged but the District Council planning department was strongly in favour of the project and, like most planning departments, wasn't interested in the views of local people. A task force was hastily convened to discuss ways of opposing the development. We also had the support of most of the shop owners in our nearby market town who were less than enthusiastic about a large chain store draining business out of their high street.

The meeting came up with all the usual ideas, a petition to the local MP, a solicitor to represent us at the planning committee, some of the more active people even talked about lying down in front of the bulldozers, but you could tell from the rising levels of righteous anger that no-one really thought we had a hope in hell. We'd all been around too long to believe that democracy actually works in practice.

That was the moment when Newt got to his feet.

"If I might have the attention of the meeting," he declaimed in a voice that could probably be heard in our County Town. "I would just like to check on the precise location of this proposed mon … stros … ity."

The last word was stretched out so it took on the air of bubonic plague.

"I presume it is those old fields out to the west we are discussing, the ones with the blackthorn and elder hedge around them and the stream along one side."

"That's right," said Marjorie Fawcett who was chairing the meeting, "they apparently belong to a Mr Griffon."

"And this Mr Griffon, I believe I am correct in saying, is not a local man, is that right?

"No, I think he lives down in the south-west somewhere. I don't know that I've ever met him."

"I have," said Roger Fraser, "we've managed that land for him on a lease basis for the last thirty years or so."

"Then can't you stop this?" someone asked.

"Wish I could," said Roger, "but the lease runs out next quarter day and Griffon has already said he won't renew it. I never thought he would get planning permission but there you go."

"I would not wish to interfere with any form of farming," said Newt, "but building cannot even be on the agenda."

Suddenly everyone was interested. "Why not?" asked Marjorie.

"It is hallowed ground," declaimed Newt, "there's a colony of serotine bats nesting there, at least one barn owl and then there's the crested newts and they're a protected species."

"Crested newts? Down there, are you sure?" asked Rupert.

"Of course I am," said Newt, "with a name like

mine I have always taken a special interest in these friendly, but sadly increasingly rare, little amphibians. Many's the time on a summer's evening I've sat by a babbling brook and—"

"Yes, yes, very interesting," said Marjorie knowing as we all did, that once launched into a dramatic flight of fancy Newt could go on for hours. "Well, this certainly puts a different slant on the matter."

Newt bowed to the chairman and sat down to a brief round of applause.

"Are you sure there are crested newts along that stream?" asked Rupert who was sitting next to him.

"No idea," muttered Newt, "but if they aren't there now, then they bloody soon will be."

It was the newts that won the day, aided by a sudden discovery of a very rare wild flower and more hitherto unheard of butterflies than you could shake a stick at. But the newts were the star of the show. Faced with a battery of opposition from every wildlife and conservation group in the county, Briscoe's withdrew. The fact, leaked to the press, that the wife of one of the District Councillors turned out to work for Briscoe's probably also helped but in any case Newton Flotman had found his new nickname. He became known as "Old Crested" and his place as a village character was assured.

It was shortly after this that Mabel finally pedalled

off to the great cycle shed in the sky, leaving Newt to inherit her cottage, her garden shed and her beloved tricycle.

Left alone, Old Crested née Newt blossomed. He did not share his mother's alleged desire to convert base metals into gold but he was a practical man with a vivid imagination. He transformed his mother's old cottage by building his own generator to give himself electricity independent of the national grid. He constructed a large gauge model railway in his garden on which he ran his own hand-built steam locomotives. This was an irresistible attraction to boys of all ages throughout the village. Give him a pile of scrap material and he could always turn it into something useful so in a way he did achieve what his mother, and his namesake, had failed to do.

But in spite of this skill it was his inventions that really set him apart though here his imagination frequently veered off track. He was a cheerful man, blessed – or cursed depending on your point of view – by an unquenchable sense of optimism and he was convinced that one day his unusual and off-the-wall ideas would make him rich and famous.

One of his first inventions was the 24-hour sundial – an ordinary sundial with a lamp mounted above it which revolved using a clockwork motor so that the lamp cast a shadow down onto the table to show the time. He proudly announced it as, "The sundial that works on cloudy days and at night", apparently completely oblivious to the anomaly in that statement.

And then there were his self-righting wellington boots. He became obsessed with the idea that whenever you took off your wellies they inevitably fell over, spreading mud where you didn't want it. He contrived a kind of swinging counter-balance made up of old fishing nets and ball bearings which, when attached to the Wellington boot, managed to make sure that it always stayed upright. Unfortunately, it also made the boot very heavy so it was quite tiring to walk in them so most people decided that a bit of mud was a small price to pay for wellie comfort.

The next innovation was an adapted electric kettle which produced a tinny rendition of *"A Life On The Ocean Wave"* when the kettle actually boiled. "Lets you know it's ready so it don't boil over," said Old Crested proudly. When it was pointed out to him that most electric kettles switched themselves off when they were ready he was completely unabashed. "Ah, but if you don't know when it switches itself off, then by the time you discover it the water be cold again. With my device you can be sure it's always hot."

Over time, Old Crested became associated with the range of imaginative but useless inventions that he was constantly producing and many of us forgot that underneath he was really quite a skilful engineer. However, we were reminded of this in quite a spectacular way in the year of the Roman invasion.

Most villages have some kind of annual event, of course, but over the years ours has acquired a reputation for being different. We call it a 'carnival' rather than a fete because as well as all the usual stalls, sideshows, beer tent and refreshments and so on, we have ... Events.

Some of these are much loved regulars like the children's sports, ferret racing and the competitions for knobbly knees (ladies only) and for the men – the most attractive person in a bikini. Others are more ad-hoc and vary in complexity and imagination from year to year. One year we had a homemade soapbox car race when most of the contestants ended up in the river. Another time we had a 'who has the biggest rabbit' competition which was made more interesting by the rules which stated the entered animal did not actually have to be a rabbit so long as it looked roughly like one. We had some very surprised cows in the village that year.

The carnival is normally held in one of Roger's fields on the bank of the river to the west of the church.

On this particular occasion it was Harry's turn to be Event Organiser and he decided on a re-enactment. He chose Boudicca versus the Romans, and to make sure we had plenty of room to manoeuvre, he arranged with Roger to use another of his fields. As he put it: "We don't want Boudicca's chariots veering off course and rampaging through the tea tent or the Roman soldiers tramping over the ferrets."

He couldn't find an affordable re-enactment society that did Boudicca and the Romans so, true to the spirit of our village, he decided we would mount our own. He called for volunteers to make up the two armies and after a bit of arm-twisting, some of which involved bribes of the kind that increased the profits in the pub, he managed to assemble a group of around thirty. There was a fair amount of squabbling as everyone wanted to be in Boudicca's army and no-one wanted to be a Roman but Harry was ruthless and arbitrarily divided the group into two.

As so often happens in small communities, fiction became reality and for a few weeks before the carnival, loyalties were split. 'Romans' refused to be seen drinking with the 'Iceni' in the pub and insults were hurled across the street from opposing warriors. Both sides tried to bolster their chances by attempting to recruit more warriors to their respective armies. Old Crested was approached by both sides but refused to join either.

"Don't hold with either of them," he said. "Bloody Italians and bloody Celts. In my opinion what they needs is a proper old Englishman to sort them out."

His listeners took this to be a casual throw-away comment and it was only later that we realised that he'd actually been completely serious.

As the date of the carnival drew nearer the excitement mounted and it was clear that attendance at this year's fete was going to be a record-breaking one. Dan at The Spy ordered extra casks of cider, the ferrets were groomed to within an inch of their lives and the Romans and the Iceni continued to snarl at each other whenever they met.

The day finally arrived. The weather was kind, there were record crowds, record takings, the barbecue was very popular, the beer tent was thronged. But then came the time for the re-enactment and suddenly the carnival was on a downhill path. Harry's group of thirty combatants had seemed fine on paper but in reality two armies of fifteen people each didn't look so impressive in the middle of a field. There was also the question of costumes. For the Romans swords were easily contrived out of a couple of pieces of wood and tin foil was pressed into service for breastplates but shields were more a problem.

"Twenty years ago we'd've used dustbin lids,"

muttered Harry, "but no-one has dustbins any more and you can't have the Roman army charging into battle with a wheelie bin held out in front of them."

Helmets were also tricky. The local pheasants learned to move very quickly to avoid their feathers being pressed into service for helmet adornment and for some weeks after the event many a housewife lamented the loss of a favourite saucepan.

Costumes for the Iceni were easier, with much employment of woollen clothing and body painting, but the chariots proved to be a real stumbling block. In the end Harry resorted to a mass purchase of old prams off E-Bay but, apart from sticking wheels and rust, it meant that the Iceni army was halved in one swoop, as each pram required one warrior inside it brandishing a sword and trying to hang on while their partner tried to push the pram at speed over the rough turf of the field.

The result was a rapid and overwhelming victory for the Romans which had not been the plan at all and offended just about everyone, except the Romans themselves who behaved like a 4th division football team which had just won the FA Cup.

The whole thing was over in less than five minutes which the crowd clearly thought was completely unsatisfactory, so Harry, faced with disaster, thought very quickly, then grabbed a megaphone and addressed the crowd.

"Right, that was the rehearsal to show you all what to do. Now comes the real thing. Everybody can join in. Everyone standing on my right is a Roman, everyone on my left joins the Iceni. Don't worry about costumes or swords, just pretend. What we need is a lot of yelling and a lot of charging."

He lowered the megaphone and mopped his brow. "I suspect this will be a shambles," he muttered to Roger, "but it might keep them quiet for a bit."

'Quiet' was not really a well-chosen word. When Harry lifted the megaphone and bellowed "Charge" absolute bedlam broke out as the two sides charged towards each other, one side led by Romans with slipping saucepans on their heads, the other by painted Iceni in rusty prams.

And then it happened. We heard the roar of the engine first and then this apparition appeared hurtling, well trundling anyway, through the field gate at a steady six miles per hour. At first glance it appeared to be a tricycle but bolted on behind it was some kind of engine which was subsequently discovered to be a truncated ride-on mower.

Perched on the tricycle, steering with one hand and holding what looked like a lance pointing skywards in the other, was a figure glad entirely in what appeared to be some kind of metal. A helmet on its head had a two narrow slits in it, one with a pair of eyes peering through, the other bellowing at full volume as the contraption puttered its way across the grass.

"Half a league, half a league, half a league onward. Into the Valley of Death rode the six hundred."

Romans and Iceni alike stopped short in their tracks as the contraption lurched towards them. Then the lance came down into the horizontal, the speed of the tricycle mower increased to around ten miles per hour and the sonorous voice declaimed: "Cry God for Harry, England and St. George."

"Nothing to do with me, this bit," muttered Harry as the whole situation swept out of control.

"Who the hell is it?" asked Jessica bewildered.

The speed on the tricycle mower was increasing rapidly now and suddenly Maureen, the landlady from The Spy, cracked the puzzle.

"It's Old Crested," she yelled, "come to save us from the Italians."

"Bit late in the day for that," said Bill.

"Yes, about fourteen hundred years too late judging by the armour he's wearing," said Nigel, "he's not exactly Boudicca, more like Lancelot of the Valley."

As we watched Old Crested, who clearly couldn't see where he was going, increased the tricycle mower speed still further and charged into the fray.

Romans and Iceni alike scattered in all directions.

"What the hell does he think he's doing", yelled Marjorie Fawcett, "someone's going to get hurt."

"Don't worry," said Rupert, "Dressed like that he can't possibly see where he's going. He won't do any damage." And he was right.

Old Crested drove wildly across the field, his lance waving uselessly around and people had plenty of time to get out of the way. He reached the fence which separated the re-enactment field from the main fête and ploughed straight through it. He missed the barbecue by a gnat's whisker then entered the beer tent by the entrance and left it through a stretch of canvas where no exit had been intended.

With an excited crowd in hot pursuit, the tricycle mower roared on towards the river. As it got there it hit a large boulder, there was a thumping crash and the motor stalled. The tricycle stopped dead but Old Crested didn't. He left the saddle, described an elegant arc through the air and landed in the river with a metallic splash that almost caused a tsunami further down in the village.

After that it was generally agreed that the carnival was over. Old Crested was fished out of the river by a group of willing and excited volunteers but there was a moment of anti-climax when it was discovered the armour was made out of flattened baked bean tins.

Old Crested was wet, chastened but even so defiant. "Well, us won that battle good a proper, didn't us," he said, but he was interrupted by a shriek from Jessica.

"Look, he's bleeding. The Romans have injured him."

We all looked and sure enough streaks of red were running down Old Crested's legs and arms.

"I'll get some water and some bandages," said Sylvia but Bill laid a hand on her arm.

"Hang on just a moment," he said. He went across to the dripping Old Crested and put his finger in the "blood" and tasted it. Then he nodded. "As I thought. Hold the panic."

He turned to Old Crested. "I don't think you washed those tins very thoroughly before you made your armour, did you?"

The truth dawned on all of us at the same time and a howl of laughter rang out as Old Crested stood there in a puddle of river water and tomato sauce.

THE HARVEST
GOAT

Visitors often perceive my Village in the Valley to be a quiet, rural community where nothing much ever happens and on the whole they're right. Not a lot does happen, but when it does it happens in style. The affair of the Harvest Goat is a case in point.

It began, like so many things in the village, quite innocuously and with good intentions on all sides.

To appreciate the background to the event it's necessary to understand the position of the church in our village. Not its physical location, more about the part it plays in village life which, these days, is pretty small. The average Sunday sees a congregation of around eight or nine people – unless any of them have guests staying in which case the duty priest may find a baker's dozen of faces staring up at him.

We don't have our own resident vicar in the village anymore. Instead, our church is part of a group of six churches under the control of one vicar, the Reverend

Victor Coggles. We don't see much of him which is quite a relief to most of us. He spends most of his time at the church in our local market town where he struts the stage as though training to be a bishop. The smaller village churches he leaves to his support team of part-time curates and lay readers, none of whom are getting any younger.

However, someone, somewhere in the mafia-like structure of our diocese must have realised that with an aging support team, reinforcements were soon going to be required, because out of the blue came the news that a new full-time curate had been appointed to assist the vicar.

But that wasn't all. Not only was she new but she was a 'her'. Rupert, whose building company does the maintenance on the main church in our local market town, told us about it in The Spy one night.

"Coggles is not a happy bunny," he said, "apparently he wasn't consulted just presented with a fait accompli."

"But surely he must be grateful for the extra help," said Jessica.

"I don't think it's the 'help' bit that concerns him," said Rupert, "more the person of the opposite gender situation."

"Oh, for heaven's sake," muttered Jessica, "what century does he think we live in?"

"Search me," said Rupert, "all I know is that he is going around muttering about 'contamination'."

The Reverend Victor Coggles has never had an easy relationship with my Village in the Valley. When he first arrived some years ago he had a battle royal with our Parochial Church Council over the style of service in our church. He wanted them to use an updated modern version, the PCC – who basically form the total congregation and not one of them under fifty – wanted to stick with the old Book of Common Prayer. Eventually they won because on the first occasion Coggles led morning service himself using the modern version, the congregation rose as a whole and walked out of the church.

"I get the impression that Coggles sees a female curate as a punishment on us," said Rupert, "especially as she's apparently chosen to live in our village."

Initially, when the news broke, there was certainly a little bit of muttering amongst the older, more traditional villagers. However, the mutterings were never serious and soon died away altogether once the Reverend Beverley Bedingham had arrived and settled in.

Her arrival was heralded by the roar of a high-powered motorbike one Saturday morning as a black leather clad figure pulled up outside the shop. The helmet was removed, the leather jacket unbuttoned to reveal first a female and then a dog collar.

"Good morning," said the apparition, "Can anyone point me towards Rose Cottage in Pond Lane?"

There was a rush of people to help. Some, mostly the blokes, wanted to examine the motor bike – a 1050cc Triumph Speedmaster. Others were just keen to see what a lady priest looked like, which was pretty much like any other lady only this one was wearing a dog collar, a Richa two-piece leather jacket and trousers with knee length leather boots and enormous gloves.

It didn't take long for the village, and not just the church goers, to realise that Beverley Bedingham was a lovely lady, human being first, curate second. She genuinely cared for her flock, not just the pew huddlers but the whole village, and set about trying to organise things that everyone could share. Of course, in these early days she was not aware of how good intentions in the village can – and so often do – spiral off into the surreal.

Bev the Rev – as she soon became known – arrived just before Easter, a bit too late to make any changes to the various events already planned. Not that this prevented her from trying. She managed to organise an Easter Egg hunt in the churchyard for the under tens but her effort to arrange a procession through the village on Palm Sunday led by a donkey was a failure.

The first problem was the reluctance of villagers to do anything so ostentatious as 'process'. Mrs Williams pleaded swollen feet, Mr Osbaldiston said he had a bad back, Vera Witheridge, a woman who gives misery a bad name, said a flat "No." The tower captain, Humphrey Snape, had a cast-iron excuse, as he had to be in the tower leading the ringers to summon people to the service, and for the same reason all the ringers were unavailable too.

Bev the Rev was a wise and sensitive lady, and she knew when she was flogging a dead donkey so she tried to downgrade the plan and just have a donkey – a live one – at the entrance to the church to welcome people to the service. Unfortunately, by this time the few donkeys in the area available for hire had already been snapped up for other Easter events. So in the end it all came to naught.

Or it would have done had it not been for Nan Mildew. Nan is a nice enough old lady, a regular church goer, though whether that's due to faith or habit is open to conjecture. Nan is always first on the doorstep with something in a pot when one of her neighbours is ill, though if you're the recipient the best course of action is to accept it politely, empty it into the dustbin, wash out the pot and return it with a kind word of thanks.

Nan thought it was very sad that the Lady Curate – as she called Bev the Rev – had been denied her donkey and she said so loudly in the shop.

"It's a real shame," she said, "her was only doing her best. What I say is, the Lady Curate needs an ass."

That statement should have been fine but by the time it had been delivered in Nan's broad dialect the alternative noun for donkey had acquired a rolling 'r' between the 'a' and the 's' which made her utterance sound rather different. Those of us in the shop at the time had to struggle to keep a straight face, but once the mirth was under control we all agreed that the Lady Curate did indeed deserve an ass or even a donkey or a mule.

"Bit late now though," said Old Crested, "Easter be done and gone for another year."

And that might have been the end of that except for Emery Jacobs who raised the subject again in the bar of The Spy that evening just as Nan walked into the bar with a jug to collect her evening cider.

"I think old Nan's right," he said, "'tis a shame the lady Rev couldn't have her donkey for Easter."

"Of course I'm right," said Nan pushing her jug across the bar to Dan.

"There's always Harvest," said Rupert thinking of the next time the congregation was likely to reach double figures.

"Don't remember anything about Jesus riding round on a donkey at harvest time," objected Sylvia, "though I do seem to remember something about his disciples helping themselves to someone else's corn."

"Mark, chapter 2, verse 23," muttered Nigel, our resident pub quiz freak.

"I was thinking more of the donkey as a beast of burden helping to bring in the harvest," said Rupert. "Perhaps we could find a donkey for Bev the Rev this autumn."

Everyone nodded and promptly forgot all about it until a week or so before the harvest festival was due when Nan accosted Rupert as he was unloading compost from the back of his car.

"When's the donkey arriving?" she asked, "and who'll be looking after it?"

"What donkey?" asked Rupert who'd completely forgotten the whole thing.

"The donkey you were arranging for the harvest festival service. The beast of burden helping to bring in the harvest, you said."

"Ah," said Rupert, as vague recollections began to stir, "that donkey."

"Yes, that donkey," said Nan remorselessly. "The donkey you promised to organise."

Rupert was pretty certain that no firm promise

had been made, only a vague idea mooted, but he knew only too well that trying to stop Nan Mildew in full flood was akin to juggling with custard on a greasy high wire in a strong wind. Something would have to be done so he raised the matter in the pub that evening.

"She's convinced I promised to arrange a donkey," he moaned, "I didn't, I'm sure I didn't, but we're going to have to find a bloody donkey from somewhere or we'll never hear the last of it."

We all noted that 'I' had become 'we' in the space of a sentence but as usual we all rallied round.

"How about that nursery down the main road," asked Sylvia, "they've got a lot of animals as well as plants and I'm pretty sure they have a donkey."

"No, they don't," said Harry, "they did have but it died. They've just got alpacas now."

"There's that donkey sanctuary that's always advertising for funds in the paper. Would they help?"

"Not a chance. We tried them once before but they said their animals had already suffered enough and they weren't putting them through the trauma of a church service."

"That's all we need – atheist donkeys," muttered Nigel.

The situation wasn't helped by Vera Witheridge who with her Labrador's nose for people in trouble and her determination to pour oil on troubled flames, took every opportunity to put the boot in with remarks about people who make promises they have no intention of keeping.

Over the next few days Rupert, supported rather half-heartedly by a rapidly co-opted donkey committee, spent hours on the phone trying unsuccessfully to rustle up a donkey from somewhere but without success.

"Maybe rustle is the word," said Jessica at last, "if we can't hire one, borrow one or buy one, then maybe we need to rustle one."

"Now there's a thought," said Rupert and we should have been warned by the familiar look of concentration that appeared on his face.

For the next few days whenever any of us came across Nan Mildew we forestalled the accusing finger by assuring her with various degrees of insincerity that everything was in hand. Rupert had a plan. Rupert was fixing it.

On the Friday before the Harvest Festival service the donkey committee gathered in The Spy. Rupert was late and some of us were on our second drink before he made an appearance. In response to our anxious looks he grinned.

"All fixed," he said. "Trust Uncle Rupert."

We pressed him for details, all keen to know

where he had managed to acquire a donkey, a breed which seemed to have taken on a scarcity that no-one who had not endured rationing in the 1940s could imagine.

Rupert had the grace to look a trifle embarrassed. "Well, it's not actually a donkey as such …" he said, and in response to our glares went on rapidly, "… well, you all know how difficult that's proved so I moved on to the next best thing."

"What is the next best thing?" asked Sylvia speaking for us all.

"I've got a goat," said Rupert proudly, "in fact I've gone one better, I've got two goats."

There was a silence as those amongst us who had once read the Bible tried to imagine Jesus riding into Jerusalem on a goat.

"Don't be silly," said Rupert testily, "that was Easter. Of course it would have to be a donkey if it were Easter but this isn't Easter, it's Harvest Festival. Produce of the field and all that."

We pointed out that a goat could hardly be called produce.

"But it lives in a field," said Rupert, "and it gives milk and stuff and what's milk if it's not produce?"

We had to acknowledge the milk argument but some of us remembered rather uneasily the light that had come into Rupert's eyes when Sylvia had made the joke about rustling.

"I suppose they are, um, how can I put this … legal goats?" asked Nigel.

"Of course, they're legal," said Rupert, rather nettled, "it was Jessica talking about rustling gave me the idea. In fact, I thought I'd better act quickly before one of you mad sods went and nicked someone's donkey or something."

Jessica opened her mouth in amazement but Rupert went straight on. "You know Russell Longstaff who used to live over by the brewery?"

We all nodded. "Well, I remembered that when he retired and moved to that bungalow in town he had the bright idea of getting a couple of goats to save him having to cut the lawn." We all nodded again. "Well, it didn't work out. The grass wasn't enough for them and it cost him a fortune in food and they destroyed the lawn with their hooves. I knew he wanted to get rid of them so I offered to help him out. They're in my garage at the moment."

There didn't seem much to say to that. It was true that goats weren't donkeys but then the relevance of a donkey to Harvest Festival had always been a bit strained so maybe goats would do fine. So long as they satisfied Nan Mildew we were content.

"One other thing," said Rupert, "keep this to yourselves for the moment. I thought it could be a nice surprise for Nan and Bev the Rev on Sunday morning."

And there we left it. On Saturday the church goers in the village, aided by the children and the nostalgia brigade, spent the day decorating the church with flowers, corn sheaves (one real, most artificial) and an assortment of produce, some from the fields and gardens, most from the supermarket in town.

Sunday was a warm, welcoming sort of day so when Humphrey Snape and his merry band were swinging on their bell ropes, I decided that just for once I would attend the service and see these harvest goats for myself. Judging by the number of people making their way through the lych gate and up the gravel path to the church door, many of the other villagers felt the same.

We settled into our pews and looked around us. There were flowers in all apertures and on every shelf, piles of produce around the alter, spilling over into the nave. It was an impressive sight, but no sign of any goats or of Rupert. It wasn't until everyone was settled, the last toll of the bell was dying away and Bev the Rev was walking in from the vestry that we heard the loud creak of the church door.

We all swung round to see Rupert standing there, a piece of rope clutched in each hand and on the end of each rope – a goat. There was a collective gasp of admiration. Rupert was dressed in his grandfather's old farming smock and wearing a straw hat with a feather in it and both goats had bright red ribbons round their neck. Just for a moment it made a magnificent picture.

But only for a moment. Rupert took a tentative step forward but as he did so the goats scented the flowers and produce, and their response was to charge. For those who don't know, a goat with its eyes on a meal is like a battering ram – down the aisle they came at breakneck speed, Rupert clutching desperately at the ropes and yelling at them to stop. When they reached the altar rail one swung north and one swung south and Rupert was hurled over the rail to land in a pile of corn sheaves at the feet of Bev the Rev.

Instantly the church was in uproar, everyone tried to make a grab for one of the trailing ropes, but the goats were intent on a late breakfast and rebuffed all attempts to stop them. They tore through the display like a combine through a cornfield and what they didn't eat they kicked sideways with their hooves.

It was a good fifteen minutes before they were finally cornered. Bill brought one down with a flying rugby tackle which any Six Nations team would have been proud of and the other was chased into the bell tower where it attempted to climb the spiral stairs only to find that cloven hooves and curvy concrete steps are not a good mix and so it fell back into the arms of Sylvia. Neither the goat nor Sylvia enjoyed the experience.

By the time a dishevelled and irritated Rupert led his still munching charges out of the church the whole place was a wreck. A shortened version of the service then took place for those who wanted to stay, but for many of us anything else would have been an anti-climax and we adjourned to the car park opposite the shop where we excitedly told each other what had happened while we waited for the pub to open.

Rupert was slightly mollified when he discovered that one of the goats had managed to chew up Vera Witheridge's handbag, but Bev the Rev took it all in her stride. She was overheard to say to one of the churchwardens that it was just as well there weren't any sheep there too, as separating the sheep from the goats that morning would have been one step too many.

No-one knows what happened to the goats. They vanished off the village radar so to speak. I have my own view of course, based on the fact that three weeks after the Harvest Festival Service the village held a Guy Fawkes bonfire on the Green, a wonderful occasion billed as fun for all the family with a hog roast. Meat in rolls there certainly was but, personally, I never saw the pig. I drew my own conclusions.

THE LONE
STRANGER

It's a well known fact that members of a family might fight themselves to a standstill behind their own front door, but let any outsider level some kind of criticism and they will instantly unite against a common enemy.

My Village in the Valley is a bit like that.

Quarrelling is one thing. Someone objects to the noise their neighbour's dog makes, someone else gets wound up about a piece of inconsiderate parking, but such things are the ebb and flow of village life, no need to take them too seriously. They will pass. Something else will come along.

Humiliation, though, is something different.

Some while back, an article about crime prevention appeared in local paper. It was a generic article written by a local PR firm, and it had some good, if obvious, advice about security lights, marking valuables, not leaving doors unlocked and so on. All fairly innocuous, or it would have been had it not mentioned by name an elderly gentleman in our village who had done none of these things and whose house had been burgled.

The magazine editor, when challenged, maintained that this had been printed by mistake. The information had been used by the writer to illustrate the point but was not intended for print. But printed it had been, causing the man a lot of distress. It also upset a lot of other people who resented this criticism from an outsider.

In this day and age, when it is the fashion for television programmes to set out to deliberately humiliate people – cooks, gardeners, singers whatever – you might think that an article in a local newspaper was neither here nor there. However, this was one of ours who had been attacked and the village didn't like it.

All of which might help to explain the instant closing of ranks on the night the Lone Stranger came to town, bursting into The Spy, in a perfect parody of a gunslinger entering a saloon.

The proper name of our village pub is *The One-Armed Spyglass* but life's too short to use that in everyday conversation. To us it's The Spy, a real pub, not one of these fancy restaurants pretending to be a pub and looking askance at people who don't order at least 3 courses with a couple of bottles of wine. The Spy is a friendly place, for locals and visitors alike.

Mostly.

Dan and Maureen Argent, who own the pub, were both born locally and what they don't know about this village and its inhabitants isn't worth knowing. But knowing isn't the same as telling and the gossip that flows around the main bar in The Spy always comes from the customers not the landlord.

"A publican is a bit like a priest," Dan is fond of saying. A remark, incidentally, which infuriates our vicar, the Reverend Victor Coggles, but causes great amusement to the curate Bev the Rev.

"Yep, a pub's like a confessional," says Dan. "We hear the lot in here and repeat none of it."

"Not unless seriously provoked," says Maureen.

"True," says Dan, "not unless seriously provoked."

On this particular evening there were about twenty people in the bar which wasn't bad for a wet Tuesday in November. As well as the usual group of locals, there were a number of visitors all tucking into a range of Maureen's magnificent bar meals. Over by the fire Old Falstaff was sitting in his usual high backed wooden chair, his fox terrier, Moonshine, asleep at his feet. As usual there were several conversations going on, ebbing and flowing, mixing and merging, when suddenly the door was thrust open with a loud crash and an apparition entered.

All conversation stopped abruptly. It wasn't just

the noise of the ill-treated door but the fact that the man did not so much come in as make an entrance. His physical presence itself was striking. He was dressed in a pair of brightly coloured blue and red check trousers which were clearly fighting a losing battle with the orange shirt which he wore under a black leather waistcoat. At his neck was a green cravat and on his head was what can only be described as a leather Stetson. As far as we could see he wasn't wearing a gun belt but that would have completed the picture of a fantasy gunslinger from a wild west show.

The stranger had clearly expected to make an impression as he paused for a moment to make sure we all had a chance to see him before advancing towards the bar, hand held out.

"Good evening, landlord," he said, "quaint little place you've got here."

Dan retreated back from the bar, ignoring the outstretched hand. Not a handshake on the first date man, is our Dan.

"Good evening," he said, "what can I get you?"

The stranger didn't answer. He simply lent on the bar and let his gaze roam round the room as though he were waiting for a glass of whiskey to come sliding along the counter towards him.

"Rather a poky little place," he observed, "but

you could probably do wonders with it if you turned it into a themed wine bar."

It was probably that remark that sealed his fate. We are always happy to welcome visitors to our village, but we don't like being patronised and you could feel a stiffening of anger run through us all.

"Do you want a drink?" asked Dan coldly, showing remarkable restraint.

"I'll have a pint of your finest ale, landlord," said the man.

"It's all fine," said Dan.

"Then you choose. I leave it to the expert."

Dan began to pull a pint – from the most expensive tap the more observant amongst us noticed – while the stranger, still leaning against the bar in a parody of every B-movie western we'd ever seen, surveyed the rest of us.

"Well, now," he said, "I bet you're all surprised to see me here."

We looked at each other. We were certainly surprised but more because of his discourteous behaviour and outlandish dress sense than for any other reason. However, it was clear that he expected to be recognised – the smug air of self-satisfaction was unmistakeable.

I caught Harry's eye, saw the glint as he nodded to Rupert and sat back in my chair to await the fun.

"We certainly are surprised, in fact completely dumfounded", said Harry using the voice that had made Parish Council chairmen duck for cover.

"Thought so," said the stranger, "and you'll never guess why I'm here."

"We're surprised," said Harry, ignoring the last question.

"Not to say dumfounded," added Rupert.

"Definitely dumbfounded," continued Harry, "as we were actually expecting Clint Eastwood."

Clearly this was not the answer the stranger was expecting. He had already opened his mouth to utter his next banal statement but then closed it again. You could almost hear his solitary brain cell whirring into action.

There was a pause while we all smiled sweetly at him.

"Clint Eastwood?" he enquired at last. "Why would I be Clint Eastwood?"

"Well, you clearly aren't him, old son, are you," said Bill, "but that's who we were expecting. Sometime this month anyway. He always pops in sometime in November, doesn't he, Dan?" And he nodded towards Dan who having pushed the pint of beer towards the stranger, was leaning forward, arms crossed on the bar.

Not a muscle on Dan's face moved. He just

nodded slowly.

"Clint Eastwood? Here?"

"Why not?" said Jessica joining in the fun, "he does own this pub after all."

"He does what?"

"I though everyone knew that. He likes bars. Clint has a bar, saloon, whatever you call it in Carmel in California, this pub and another one in … oh, where was it now?"

"Macedonia," said Rupert with a completely straight face. "A little village called Dobroshane. Apparently the local wine there is out of this world".

The stranger, slightly deflated, looked round at us all. He was clearly fairly certain he was having his leg pulled but not quite certain enough to challenge us. Nigel decided to join in.

"So the question is," said Nigel, "if you're not Clint Eastwood …"

"And the trousers prove that," said Jessica.

"Quite. So if that's the case, the question is why are you impersonating Clint Eastwood?"

"I'm not impersonating Clint Eastwood," said the stranger desperately, "I am Marcus Leatherbridge."

We all looked blank.

"You must know me," said the stranger, "Marcus Leatherbridge, you know, 'Strange Ways Of The World'."

Harry shook his head slowly. "Doesn't ring any bells," he said, "I think you must have come on the wrong night. Quiz night's Fridays."

"Every other Friday," said Dan from behind the bar.

"My mistake," said Harry, "Of course it's every other Friday."

"And it's not this Friday," said Dan.

"No, that's right," said Bill, "so if you're the new quizmaster you're a week and three days too early."

The stranger's initial arrogant confidence had all but gone. "I am not the new quiz master," he said, "I am Marcus Leatherbridge. I'm a television celebrity."

There was a brief pause and then Sylvia spoke for us all.

"How sad," she said, "you have our sympathy."

"Sympathy, what do you mean – sympathy?"

"Well," said Sylvia, "the modern definition of a celebrity is a talentless nonentity who uses smoke and mirrors to pretend the sum of their parts is greater than the whole."

"That's right," said Nigel, determined to join in, "like that children's story 'The Emperor's New Clothes'."

"Exactly," said Jessica, "all bluff and no substance."

There was a brief silence as we watched Marcus Leatherbridge's brain cell click into action again. Then to our surprise he laughed.

"Gee, you guys, really had me going there for a moment. I really thought you didn't recognise me."

It may be that some in the room did but if so they were not letting on.

"Don't be silly," said Rupert, "of course we recognised you. You're one of those clowns on that CBeebies show – the *'Twinkle Fairy Village'*. My little grand-daughter watches that."

"No, I'm—"

"Don't be daft," said Sylvia scornfully. "He's the guy who does the advert for edible washing powder."

"No, I'm—"

"Think you're wrong," said Harry, "I'm sure I've seen him on that *'True Confessions of a Car Wash Mechanic'* programme. Are you the guy who pretends to do oil changes with Lucozade?"

"No, I'm not," howled the stranger. "For God's sake, I'm the presenter of *'Strange Ways of the World'*."

There was a short silence, then Bill shook his head. "Never heard of it," he said.

"Nor have I," said Sylvia.

"Nor me," said Rupert, "is it a comedy programme of some kind?"

At this point the fox terrier Moonshine raised his head from where he'd been asleep at Old Falstaff's feet by the fire and let out a mournful wail. We all turned towards the sound and Falstaff – never one to miss the chance of a quote from Shakespeare – stuck in his two-pennorth. "As the bard made the great King Harry say," he declaimed, "The empty vessel makes the loudest sound."

"It's the greatest sound, not the loudest," muttered Jessica, "and it was one of the minor characters, not Henry the Fifth."

We're all used to Old Falstaff and his quotations and mostly we just nod and smile politely but in the circumstances this was too good an opportunity to miss so we all piled in.

"Ah, yes," said Bill, "there's plenty of sound in an empty barrel."

"A barrel full of certainties won't roll very far," added Sylvia.

"Roll out the barrel," added Rupert hopefully delivering the only 'barrel' quote he could think of.

But it seemed that Old Falstaff hadn't finished. "I know he," he announced waving his unlit pipe in the direction of the stranger. "He's that fella off the tele that goes around making folks look stupid."

All eyes swivelled to Marcus Leatherbridge. "Now, come on", he said, "that's not quite a fair description."

At this point landlady Maureen entered the fray. "Seems a fair enough description to me," she said. "I saw the rubbish you did in that village over in Wales. Little kids in smocks dancing round a maypole. Load of old cobblers."

"They had a great time," protested Marcus, "they were all volunteers."

Maureen sniffed – and Maureen's sniffs were legendary. "Ice creams and backhanders to the parents, I don't doubt," she said. "Well fair enough if folks are that stupid, but to make out that maypole dancing was a traditional Welsh practice, well, that's downright dishonest."

"Television scraping the top of the barrel," said Jessica completing the quotation contest.

Self-deluded waste of space he might have been, but Marcus was no quitter. "Look," he said, "I don't think you guys understand. You've got a great little village here, pub with a funny name, lots of cute characters …" he inclined his head towards Old Falstaff, "quaint old houses with wood stuck all over them. This place is a natural for *Strange Ways of the World*. It just needs a bit of branding."

There was a silence as we contemplated the appalling prospect of televised maypole dancing on our village green and The Spy becoming a themed wine bar but Marcus seized the opportunity to re-establish the initiative.

"Well now," he said, "we can talk about all that later. You're just going to love the plans I've got for this dinky little village of yours. In the meantime, now I'm here I was thinking of having something to eat."

We shook ourselves and glanced at each other in anticipation of what was to follow. Maureen was famous for her simple but tasty bar meals but like all artists she was temperamental and she had clearly taken a dislike to Marcus Leatherbridge.

"If you wish," she said frostily, "you can have anything you want so long as it's ham, egg and chips."

"Can I see a menu?"

"Don't have a written one," said Dan, pushing the days' menu quickly out of sight, "most people can remember ham, egg and chips."

"Is that all you do?"

"There's sandwiches. Cheese, or ham, or cheese and ham, or ham and cheese. Or beetroot."

The stranger looked nonplussed. "Beetroot."

"Beetroot sandwiches. Very popular. With or without hedgehog pickle."

Dan kept a perfectly straight face as he said this and most of us managed to do the same, though Nigel did make a fast exit to the loo.

There was a brief pause then Marcus nodded down the far end of the room where a party of four were finishing what was clearly a substantial meal. "What are they having?"

"Pre-ordered," said Dan without a pause. "So

what's it to be then?"

Marcus clearly knew when he was on a loser. "Fine, I'll have one round of ham and one round of cheese sandwiches. Do you have any mustard for the ham?"

Maureen shook her head. "No mustard. Just hedgehog pickle. Or I could do you a few fried radishes in brown sauce."

Marcus swallowed. "Just the sandwiches, thank you."

Maureen disappeared into the kitchen and Marcus turned back to the rest of us.

"Now then," he said, "let's get down to business. I'm here to do a preliminary recce of this village. I like to do my own research and set up my own contacts. So who's the head honcho round here?" He laughed. "Who do I have to treat to a beetroot sandwich in order to get access to everything."

For a moment there was a silence then Harry nodded thoughtfully. "You'll be wanting the squire," he said.

"The squire? You mean you have a squire? I thought, maybe the chairman of the Parish Council or something."

Harry shook his head. "No, the Parish Council has no power. They're all in thrall to the squire. Round here it's him who decides things."

"Well, okay then, who is this squire and how do I get hold of him?"

"Well now," said Harry, "you might just be in luck there. I am one of the few people that's allowed to speak to him and I might just be able to persuade him to come down here and meet you, seeing it's for the telly like."

Harry's attempt at talking in the local accent was appalling but Marcus didn't seem to notice.

"Well, that would be great," he said, "What's his name?"

"Roger Fraser," said Harry with straight face. "I could go and give him a ring now if you want."

"Wonderful," said Marcus draining his glass and pushing it over the bar to Dan for a refill. "Let's get on with it."

While his back was turned the rest of us exchanged glances. Harry was clearly up to something. Roger was certainly one of the main landowners round here but he'd have laughed like a drain if anyone had called him 'squire'. And Marjorie Fawcett, the Parish Council chairman, would not have liked being told she had no power.

A few minutes later Harry came back into the bar rubbing his hands together. "All fixed," he said, "Squire'll be along in a few minutes."

"That's great," said Marcus, "What sort of man

is he?"

"Well," said Harry, "he's always been a little strange. Rather power mad you know. Has been known to shoot at trespassers on his hand."

"He does what?"

"Oh, he never hits them. He's a lousy shot for a squire. But he occasionally hits things that he's not aiming at. If you see the squire with his gun the safest place to be is in front of him, not off to one side."

"But even if he doesn't hit them, isn't shooting at people against the law?"

By now we were all cottoning on to Harry's game so Nigel chipped in quickly. "It may be against the law in other places but the squire is the law round here. It'd be a brave policeman who showed his face in this village."

"And he's a little more brusque than usual at the moment," said Harry, "on account of the fact that his wife fell into the combine harvester last month so he's been having to cook for himself."

Marcus cast him a sharp look but Harry's face was as straight as a poker. At that moment the pub door opened and Roger walked in.

"Ah, well, now," said Harry in an accent that would have got him kicked out of any drama school, "here be the squire now."

Roger had clearly been well briefed by Harry.

He was wearing the most appalling check jacket with a pair of trousers that a jumble sale would have refused. On his head was a greasy cloth cap pulled down rakishly on one side.

Marcus moved to greet him. "Good evening, squire," he said holding out his hand.

"Evening," grunted Roger, making no move to take it. "Gather you want to talk to me, what!"

"Well, yes, I do, but first, can I get you a drink?"

"Pernod and brandy cocktail with a single olive, shaken and not stirred."

Marcus looked rather taken aback but he nodded to Dan who began mixing things in a glass.

"Well, my name is Marcus Leatherbridge, you've probably heard of me." He paused hopefully but there was no response from Roger. "Okay, well, I present this television programme 'Strange Ways Of The World' and we'd like to make a programme about this village."

Roger accepted the glass that Dan was offering him and sniffed it suspiciously. "Needs three more drops of Pernod," he said, pushing it back across the bar.

"So what do you think?" said Marcus. "It could really put this village on the map."

"On the map already," grunted Roger, "can show you the Ordinance Survey sheet if you don't believe me."

"No, no, what I meant was … Well, never mind. What do you think about featuring this village? I'll need access to the main buildings, some of the residents, all the various groups and organisations of course and—"

"Great idea," grunted Roger, accepting the glass Dan was offering him.

"Good, well in that case—"

"How much?"

"Oh, I see, um, well of course we'll pay the village a facility fee."

"To hell with the village," grunted Roger pushing the glass back towards Dan. "Needs another olive."

"What do you mean, 'to hell with the village'?"

"Don't give a stuff about the village. But my pheasant shoot will need restocking next season and my large greenhouses could do with replacing."

"Now just a minute—"

"I can let you have the number of my Swiss bank account if you pop round tomorrow. In fact, why don't you join us for a pheasant shoot. I'm taking my gun out in the morning. You're welcome to come along."

Behind Roger's back Marcus could see Harry frantically waving and mouthing "No, it's not safe."

"Well, that's very kind of you," said Marcus, "but

I'm afraid—"

"No need to be afraid," said Roger, "I haven't shot anyone for over a fortnight now. Must be a record." And he glared round at us all and we all nodded frantically in agreement.

Dan came round the bar holding a small tray with a glass nestling on a napkin.

"Ere be your drink, squire," he said attempting to pull his non-existent forelock without dropping the tray, "I do trust it's to your liking this time."

Roger took the glass, sniffed it, took a cautious sip and then with a violent motion leaned over the bar and poured the contents down the sink.

"Call that a Pernod cocktail," he roared, "it's disgusting. I've a damn good mind to shut this place down."

Dan dropped to his knees in front of Roger. "Oh, no sir, please sir, don't do that sir."

Bill stepped forward and helped Dan to his feet. "Why don't you go and join Maureen," he said, "While I try and sort this out."

Nigel came forward and helped Bill ease Roger off to one side, Marcus looking on, mouth agape.

"I don't think this is a good moment," said Harry. "I'm not sure you're going to get much co-operation from him at the moment."

"No, you damn well won't," yelled Roger,

breaking free from Bill's restraining arm, "your Pernod cocktails are rubbish. Where's my gun, did I leave it in the Land Rover?"

"He's only joking," said Harry unconvincingly, "but frankly I think it would be best if you left."

"Yes," said Marcus, "I think you're right. I don't think this village really fits our requirements."

"You could always try one of those villages to the south just over the county border," said Sylvia, "they're definitely quaint down there."

"Thanks, I might just do that," said Marcus, "Look, here's twenty quid for the drinks and sandwiches. Share them amongst yourselves if they ever arrive."

He moved to the door and looked round for a moment. "What a place," he said regretfully, and he was gone.

There was a collective sigh of relief in the bar, then we crowded round Harry and Roger, congratulating them.

Roger grinned. "I quite enjoyed it actually," he said, "I was nodding off in front of a documentary on Peruvian art when Harry rang. This was much more fun."

"Quick thinking, Harry old son, said Bill, "come on let's get another round in. What will it be, Roger, another Pernod cocktail?"

"I'll settle for a pint," said Roger as Dan emerged from the kitchen with a rare grin on his face.

The drinks were nicely lined up on the bar when suddenly the pub door opened and to our dismay Marcus Leatherbridge appeared again.

We all froze. He stood in the doorway and looked round at us.

"Just wanted to mention," he said, "that I loved the performance. Really impressive. I still think you're making a mistake but I know when I'm beat. If I don't have your cooperation then we can't make a good programme so I'll go elsewhere." He nodded to Roger. "Evening, squire. Enjoy the beetroot."

And he went out and shut the door behind him.

A BRIDGE OVER
TROUBLED WATERS

They say that if a butterfly waggles its wings in China then a hurricane will sweep through the Amazon rain forest or something like that. I've never been totally convinced by this idea but there is no doubt that sometimes a casual event can lead to a momentous change.

This is especially true in my Village in the Valley where the unusual is never unusual and rural myths are regularly born. A good example would be the time when Emery Jacobs was knocked into a ditch and so, indirectly, solved the village hall parking problem.

What actually happened, before the village myth makers got hold of it, was that Emery, having been to a Bingo night in the village hall, was staggering home in the dark. Back then, to get to the main village from the hall you had to walk down an unlit lane, cross the narrow road bridge over the river and then along the main street until the lights of the houses were close enough to offer some guidance. There are no streetlights in our village.

On this particular evening, Emery was just crossing the bridge when a car slightly misjudged the space and clipped him with its wing mirror. The car was not moving fast and the driver probably didn't even know it had happened, but Emery was caught sufficiently off balance to tumble over and fall down the bank. Fortunately he didn't fall into the main river but into the drainage ditch that comes down from the allotments into the main stream. There wasn't much water in the ditch so, although he was covered in mud, he wasn't hurt and Harry and Sylvia who were just behind him soon pulled him out. They helped him back to the village, parked him by the fire in the main bar of The Spy and restored him with a couple of stiff brandies.

Old Falstaff, in his customary place by the hearth with his fox terrier, Moonshine, at his feet, had his own comment to make – inevitably.

"What fates impose, that men must needs abide;
It boots not to resist both wind and tide."

As Jessica wasn't there we had no idea which Shakespeare play that came from and the 'woof' from Moonshine at the end of the quote was not very illuminating. It did irritate Emery though.

"Nothing to do with fate," he said, "and there bain't be no tide in that river."

As an incident it was very minor. But by next morning the story was that a car going too fast had hit Emery Jacobs on the bridge and he now had a broken arm and could hardly walk. That story spread rapidly, not hindered at all by the sight of Emery trotting along the village street doing his shopping as usual with both arms clearly functioning.

A more positive outcome of the Emery bridge incident was to reignite the discussion about access to the village hall.

Our hall is a lovely building, converted from an old barn which was donated to the village at the time of the coronation in 1953. The conversion was done by a team of volunteer village craftsmen and the result is a very attractive meeting place for functions such as Parish Council meetings, the pre-school play group, church coffee mornings, whist drives, village quizzes, harvest suppers and all the events that occur in a small community like ours.

The only snag is that it's on the other side of the river to the main village and there's no parking available at the hall, just a couple of slight indents on the verge which can be used for brief stops to unload supplies. The lane itself is edged with old flint walls that encase the fields so there's no scope for improving the situation. Parking in the village the other side of the river is not a problem. There's a perfectly good car park in the main street which serves both the village and the pub, but to park there for the village hall means a walk along the road to the bridge, over the river and then back along the lane. Not too bad on a nice evening in summer but less good on a dark winter's night or when it's raining.

For many years this state of affairs was simply tolerated – the status quo is always the easiest option – but following Emery's unsought for baptism, some of the village hall committee began to get nervous about health and safety issues and possible claims on their already meagre funds.

This sparked animated discussion, so Hugo Framlington, the village hall chairman, asked for the question of parking at the village hall to be put on the agenda for the next Parish Council meeting. Many of us went to this meeting, swelling the normal audience of three to a respectable number.

When this item was reached Marjorie Fawcett, the Council Chairman, suspended the main meeting and opened the discussion to the floor. Marjorie is a good chairman. She doesn't believe in waffle and goes straight for the jugular. "This is a matter that concerns the whole village," she said, "we have to do something about this parking problem at the hall. We can't allow our older residents to go on being hurled willy-nilly into the mud." From which statement it can be deduced that Marjorie herself is not above a bit of hyperbole when it suits her cause.

"But there's nowhere to put a car park at the hall," said Hugo, "that's the problem."

"We don't need parking space at the hall," said Marjorie, "there's a perfectly good car park in the village. It's the river that's the trouble."

"Literally troubled waters, then," muttered Sylvia.

"Trouble or not, it's there," said Nigel, "and there's nothing we can do about that."

"No, we can't," said Harry cynical as ever. "And I doubt even the few church goers in the village have enough faith to walk across the water."

Marjorie gave him a withering stare. "I wasn't suggesting that anyone should walk on or through the water," she said tersely.

For a moment the more imaginative amongst us had visions of death slides across the river with people hanging on ropes in a harness, but then sanity prevailed.

"The answer is quite simple," said Marjorie, "all we need is a footbridge across the river from the village car park and problem's solved."

There were several nods around the room from more recent residents, but Rupert shook his head.

"That's been suggested before," he said, "back in the late 60s, I think. Before your time, Marjorie."

Marjorie nodded. "So why didn't it happen?"

"District Council wasn't helpful," said Rupert laconically.

"Did they refuse permission?" asked Sylvia.

"Not in so many words," said Rupert, "but as usual they went out of their way to be obstructive. Nothing in writing, of course, it was nod, nod, wink, wink, with a list of technical requirements as long as your arm. They would only consider a planning application if we had consultants' reports, detailed plans, permission from the Environment Agency, or whatever they were called in those days, and so on and so on."

"I seem to remember they said we'd probably get permission if we used their consultant," said Roger.

"They didn't actually say that," said Rupert, "but we were being pushed pretty heavily in that direction."

"And no doubt the fact their consultant's wife was on the District Council at the time was pure coincidence," said Roger. "However, we didn't have the money so in the end I think we just gave up."

"That was a long time ago," said Hugo hopefully, "maybe things are different now."

A glance round the room showed that most of us thought that statement was a triumph of optimism over experience.

There was a short silence then from the back of the hall we heard Bill's voice.

"What we need," he said, "is a fait accompli. Leave it to me."

Bill is a retired Colonel who served in the Royal Engineers. He's a good man to know but he believes in solutions, not discussion. I thought I saw a quick glance pass between him and Marjorie, then Marjorie moved rapidly on. "Right, well if that's a non-starter there's no need to minute it," she said. "Item 7 – Footpaths Report."

And that, as far as the Parish Council was concerned, was that but it soon became clear to some of us that, whether it was minuted or not, the project was far from dead.

Over the next few days some of us were approached by Bill to form a 'footbridge task force' as he called it. Unusually we didn't meet in The Spy but in Bill's home. He has a large barn at the back of his house which he's converted into a workshop – though we understood, from an unguarded remark, that his wife calls it his playroom.

We sat around on hard wooden stools while Bill outlined his plan. "We're going to put a footbridge across the river," he announced, "without going through all that red tape rubbish. We'll make all the preparations off-site then erect the thing overnight in one hit."

"Who will?" Sylvia asked.

"I will," said Bill, "but I'll need a bit of help. But before we go any further, we need to survey the site."

Thus it was that a couple of days later the members of the Footbridge Task Force found themselves wandering around on both sides of the river, some with clipboards, others with flags. I was standing on the village hall side clutching a stick with a bit of cloth attached, moving around in response to waved instructions from Bill across the river in the village car park. Sylvia was 30 feet to the left of me, also clutching a flag, while Harry was with Bill, making notes as he called out information. It was about as subtle as a foghorn in a symphony concert but Bill was adamant that no-one would take any notice.

"Not in this village," he said, "you could lead a herd of camels through the main street and the only interest aroused would be to see who could grab the dung for their garden."

The next stage, Bill informed us, was to get the constituent parts made and for that he had enlisted the services of a garden designer who lived about thirty miles away over the county border. Bill's plan was to have the bridge delivered, in kit form as it were, and to assemble it in his workshop. Then one night, with recruited labour, the bridge would be installed.

"We may need to do a bit of final work in daylight," said Bill, "just to make sure the ends are secure but basically we'll have our fait accompli."

There were to be three basic sections of the bridge, the walkway made out of stout timbers with planks nailed across them, the handrails, also of stout timber with uprights that would be set into the ground, and the foundation upon which it would all sit.

"The ends are going to need a firm base to rest on," said Bill, "and they'll have to be prepared in advance but I've thought about that. We can sort out the end in the car park by saying we're doing repairs to the surface while actually strengthening the area where the bridge will rest."

"But what about the village hall side," asked Sylvia, "surely someone will raise an eyebrow if we start digging holes and slapping concrete down there."

"Barbecue base," said Bill triumphantly, "if anyone asks we say we're preparing a base for a permanent barbecue. No probs."

It was Nigel, our retired solicitor, who raised the obvious question. "I'm all for avoiding any contact with the District Council," he said, "but don't you think someone is going to notice a footbridge now exists where one didn't before?"

Bill and Harry exchanged satisfied glances. "We

thought of that," Harry said, "but we've solved it. We found an anorak."

"You're going to need more than an anorak to camouflage a footbridge," said Sylvia and Bill laughed.

"Not that kind of anorak, a teenage whiz kid who can make computers dance to her own tune."

"Impressive though such a sight may be," said Nigel, "how will this hide the footbridge?"

"Simple," said Bill, "it won't. There's an old army maxim, if you can't hide it, advertise it."

We all looked at him but it was Harry who came to our rescue. "Think of it like this, why aren't we going through the proper planning channels?"

"Because our experience with the District Council is that it says no to anything useful," said Sylvia, "and anyway it would take months and a lot of money to even put in an application to erect a new structure."

"That's just it," said Bill, "So, we're not going to erect a new structure. We going to repair an existing one. You don't need formal planning to restore the status quo."

We all looked at each other. "I didn't know there used to be a footbridge there," said Nigel, "I'm surprised Rupert didn't mention it."

Harry had the grace to look a bit sheepish. "Ah. Well. Rupert wouldn't have known about it."

"Why not? He's lived here since Noah wore shorts and his family were here for generations before that. Surely they'd have known about a previous footbridge."

"Well, yes, they would, only there wasn't one, so they couldn't."

"But you said—"

"Yes, yes, I know," said Bill testily, "there never actually was a footbridge here in the past but by the time my whizz kid has finished there will have been. If you see what I mean," he ended lamely.

There was a short silence.

"Let me get this straight," said Sylvia, "you're proposing we erect a brand new footbridge where there's never been one before and then you'll maintain you're replacing something that was there before even though it wasn't."

"That's it", said Harry, "good idea, isn't it?"

"But won't there be records, deeds and stuff like that."

"Possibly," said Harry, "but equally possibly not. If we date the whole exercise before the time the Land Registry started digitalising all their records, then any plans, deeds whatever may well have gone missing."

"Yes," said Bill, "you remember all the trouble we had when the Parish Council wanted to buy that land for allotments, the original deeds couldn't be found so the farmer—"

"Was that Jake Higgins?"

"Yes, Higgins – he had Hell's own trouble proving title so he could sell it to us and that is quite normal for printed deeds."

"But surely there'll be photographs, planning applications, God knows what to disprove this."

"Not by the time our whizz kid has finished," said Bill. "She's already working on the photos from the early 1900s showing a footbridge across the river next to the pub."

The Footbridge Task Force considered this statement in silence.

"So ..." said Nigel after a moment, "you're proposing to falsify the records to show there used to be a footbridge across the river at this point and so we are merely restoring it."

"Not exactly falsifying the records," said Bill, "the chances are that no-one will even notice a bridge has appeared but just in case they do we're preparing a line of defence."

"If they should challenge it," went on Harry, "then we'll be able to produce old photos showing an early version of the bridge in position, together with documents showing how permission was applied for and granted back then. Consultants' report, correspondence with the council and all that stuff. I have to say this computer lass is brilliant. She's even matched the font to make the letters look as though they were written on a 1970s Council typewriter."

It was Sylvia who made up our collective mind. "Well, I hope you're right," she said, "but we've come this far and we know we'll never get a footbridge by the proper channels so let's give this a go."

So it was that three weeks later a group of us assembled in Bill's playroom. Outside in his yard, camouflaged by a large tarpaulin, the bridge stood on one of Rupert's flatbed trucks. Bill and Harry, helped by Rupert who had been recruited to the group, had assembled it from the delivered parts. Just after midnight we trundled it down to the village and into the car park by the pub where one of Rupert's friends with his JCB was waiting for us. The windows of The Spy were dark but we knew that Dan and Maureen would be watching. Marjorie was also with us although she kept saying she wasn't.

"I'm not here. The Parish Council knows nothing about this but I've brought a flask of brandy. Anyone want a swig?"

Working as quietly as we could, the bridge was unloaded from the truck and with careful manoeuvring by the JCB driver, was swung out over the river. Bill had attached ropes to the far end and these were now hurled across what Sylvia insisted on calling 'the troubled waters' where Harry, Nigel and their group of helpers were waiting to catch them. Then with them gently pulling and the JCB edging forward, the bridge was neatly dropped into place on its new foundations and the process of fixing it in position began.

The work was finished just before dawn and tapes run across each end to prevent anyone using it before the cement holding the posts in place had completely set. Then, tired and dirty, we all adjourned to The Spy where Maureen cooked us a big fry up.

In the final stage of the plan Hugo wrote an article for the village magazine about the 'restoring' of the footbridge. He also sent press releases in a similar vein to the regional press, all of whom printed the exact words without bothering to check the facts.

For a few months we collectively held our breath waiting to see if there would be any reaction. We weren't worried about Kevin Tinker, our local District Councillor, who was so lazy he couldn't tie his own shoelaces without a team of helpers, but we did wonder if someone from the County Council might notice. But they never did.

Until about a year later when the village hall committee had a letter from the County Council suggesting that it might be wise to pin some wire netting across the walkway of the bridge to avoid a slip hazard in wet weather so we took that to mean that we were in the clear.

As Harry said: "Publicise a myth often enough and loud enough, and in a short space of time the myth becomes fact."

And he should know. He used to be in the banking industry.

THE COURSE OF
TRUE LOVE ...

I't's a truth universally acknowledged that other people's relationships, especially when they're not going smoothly, are always fascinating to those who aren't involved. I particularly remember the time, some while back now, when the village was stunned by Granfer Butterball publicly announcing that he was going to divorce his wife, Martha, on the grounds of unreasonable behaviour.

As they had been married 65 years at the time and Granfer had just turned 90 with Martha not far behind, this was news indeed. For a day or two the village was agog with rumours that Martha had been having a riotous liaison with the window cleaner but, as so often, rumour and imagination had outpaced reality. Their daughter Valerie stepped in, gave her parents a good talking to, and divorce vanished off the agenda. Much later we learned that the 'unreasonable behaviour' was due to Martha, who enjoyed watching the cooking programmes on television, trying out a new recipe which involved garlic. Granfer didn't do garlic and made his feelings about 'that foreign muck' very clear.

The question of whether Vera Witheridge was or was not married was much more interesting. Vera is one of those people who gives misery a bad name and whenever there is serious bad feeling in the village you can bet that Vera is at the bottom of it. We had always assumed that she was unmarried – which most of us found completely understandable – but then one day we were treated to the sight of Vera and an unnamed man in the carpark outside The Spy engaged in a heated argument. He appeared to be insisting that she either came home with him now or he would divorce her. She appeared to be saying that she had never seen him before in her life and she was not married to anyone. It ended with her hitting him with a box of eggs and stalking off, leaving him to wander off down the street, covered in egg yolk and muttering to himself. It was the most exciting thing that had happened since Nan Mildew's home-made wine exploded in the village hall but it did leave rather a lot of questions unanswered.

In spite of occurrences like this our village is normally a quiet sort of place but there is no doubt that when something does happen, then it happens in style. The proposed nuptials of Prunella Bracebridge certainly came into that category.

As usual when a drama erupts it often starts in The Spy. A group of us were in there one evening when suddenly the pub door was flung open violently and Philip Bracebridge appeared.

"Gently does it," said Dan, "have some respect for my door."

Philip rarely comes into The Spy so his appearance was a surprise, but we could see at a glance that he was clearly upset.

"I need a drink," were his opening words.

"Has something happened?" asked Bill rather unnecessarily as something clearly had.

"Oh, yes, something's happened," said Philip, "sorry about the door Dan, can I have a scotch please. Double."

"I'll get this," said Harry as we pulled a bar stool forward and sat Philip down. "Now then, what's the problem?"

Philip sunk half the scotch in one go, put the glass down on the bar and announced. "My daughter's getting married."

There was a silence. We hadn't expected that. The Pavlov response was obviously 'Congratulations' but the build up to the announcement suggested strongly that this would be out of place. There was a short pause then Sylvia ventured tentatively. "Is there a problem with that?"

"There won't be after she's gone," said Philip, "but there will be if I end up braining her with a mattock before the ceremony."

We took this to be a typical piece of village hyperbole but clearly the path towards matrimony was not going smoothly so Nigel bought him another double and we gently coaxed the story out him.

Prunella Bracebridge was, to put it as courteously as possible, a well-built lass with a personality that matched her physical size. Many of us still remembered the occasion when she'd been picked for her school rugby team, 14 fellas and Prunella. The opposing school had objected but they couldn't find anything in the rules that said all the team had to be boys so the game went ahead and the spectators watched with a mix of emotions as Prunella mowed down the opposing forwards like a Panzer division going through Belgium.

The news that she was getting married should have been a cause for celebration but clearly there were obstacles in the path that brute force could not iron out. Gradually, as we plied Philip with scotch, the obstacles emerged.

Prunella, now working as a games teacher at a school in our County Town, had met her opposite number at a neighbouring school. His name was Edwin and, the way Philip told it, it wasn't so much love at first sight as: "He plays sport, he'll do". The fact that Prunella's passions were rugby, soccer and hockey while Edwin's were golf, swimming and running marathons, had not prevented her proposing and the kick-off whistle was blown for a good sporting fixture.

However, Prunella was nothing if not original and the first bombshell landed when she announced she wanted a 'fairy tale wedding' and so she had chosen a Buddhist ceremony. Neither Philip, nor his wife Samantha, had the faintest idea what that meant but it sounded complicated, not the least because to the best of their knowledge, Prunella was not a Buddhist. Ever tactful they had asked what Edwin thought about it, an idea that Prunella clearly thought completely irrelevant. Samantha was all for ignoring the whole Buddhist thing but Philip felt he had a duty towards his only daughter, and so began looking into the matter. He spent several days on the internet and had amassed a wealth of information when Prunella changed her mind. She'd discovered that a Buddhist wedding meant they couldn't have Chicken à la King for the wedding breakfast which she had set her heart on so Buddhism was off.

"So what happened then?" asked Bill.

"She decided on a church wedding with all the trimmings," said Philip gloomily.

Ah, we all thought, *that'll set him back a penny or two.*

"That'll set you back a penny or two," said Jessica to whom the concept of tact was completely unknown.

"That's not the problem," said Philip, "I told her some while ago that I'd set aside a sum of money for her wedding. She could spend it all on the ceremony or she could spend some of it on that and keep the rest for the honeymoon or whatever else she wanted."

Harry nodded, ever the merchant banker. "Fixed budget," he said, "good plan."

"So she's chosen to spend it all on a posh church do, has she?" asked Sylvia.

"Not exactly," said Philip, "there's a problem with the church."

"What kind of problem?" asked Harry.

"Wrong size, wrong place, apparently," said Philip and proceeded to explain. Instead of taking the sensible route and opting for our village church with the service being taken by Bev the Rev, Prunella had decided that she wanted a fairy tale church so she'd chosen one in the next county, a little chocolate-box church with a round tower that at a pinch could seat about 40 people. Prunella had imagined you could just choose a church like a new pair of shoes and was outraged when she was told by the vicar of that parish that as a non-resident she would need to apply for special permission.

Prunella had no time for what she called 'Jobsworth bureaucracy' so she told him what he could do with his church and the whole thing was back to square one.

"Mealtimes were getting increasingly uncomfortable," said Philip. "Her mother has no patience with all this shilly-shallying and although I just want her to have a nice day, I was getting a bit fed up too."

"So what's the final outcome?" asked Sylvia.

"There isn't one. Not yet," said Philip. "That's why I needed a drink."

The next stage, he told us, was a brief flirtation with a so-called 'natural wedding'. Apparently that meant standing in a field in a kind of smock with flowers in her hair while someone played mournful harp music off an I-Pod.

"Is that actually legal?" asked Harry.

"No idea. Apparently she quite fancied it taking place on the main pitch at the local rugby club but they refused to even consider it so that got kicked into touch."

"Someone should kick her into touch," muttered Jessica darkly but we quickly shut her up as we were all keen to hear about the next development.

"Her next idea was an island in the Caribbean," said Philip, "but it didn't take long for even Prunella to realise the budget wouldn't run to that, so we came back to the church option, only this time she decided our own village church would do."

"Thank goodness for that," said Dan, pouring him another scotch. "Have this one on the house. I think you've earned it."

"Not so fast," said Philip, "that's gone belly up too. That twat of a vicar of ours said no, she wasn't a church goer and the church wasn't just there for people's convenience."

"That sounds like Victor Coggles," muttered Sylvia, "she should have gone straight to Bev the Rev."

"Well, old Coggles couldn't have been more obstructive," said Philip, "I think he'd got wind of the Buddhist thing too which probably didn't help." His head drooped. "The whole thing just goes on and on. At one stage she mentioned holding the ceremony on a 3-mast schooner off the coast but that idea came and went so quickly that we never got down to details."

"So what's the situation now?" asked Sylvia.

"Registry office," said Philip, "but even that's not straightforward. She's now decided it'd be romantic," he rolled his eyes upwards, "to get married on her birthday."

"And when's that?"

"A bit less than two months' time so. Heaven knows if we'll ever find a vacant slot in that time scale."

Bringing all this frustration out into the open clearly helped Philip as he insisted on buying a round before Harry poured him into his car and drove him home.

And that should have been that as far as the village was concerned but a few days later Philip rang Bill to say against all the odds they'd managed to book a slot in the local registry office and everything was finally set fair to go. He then, rather tentatively, asked if a few of us would be willing to come to the wedding to support him.

"Samantha's getting very cool about the whole thing," he said, "and hasn't invited many of our family. I think we're going to be outnumbered so if you could …"

Difficult to resist a plaintive plea so Bill said yes and coaxed Harry, Sylvia and myself to join him.

The wedding was to be at 4.00 pm and we all went together in Bill's car. "Keeping the support troops in tight knit formation," as Bill put it. There was a small crowd milling around the car park but no sign of Philip, Samantha or Prunella. We had no idea what the bridegroom looked like and there was no-one in conventional wedding attire so we stood in our small group waiting for something to happen.

Around ten to four there was a bustle in the crowd and a kind of Laurel and Hardy pair moved onto the steps.

"Ladies and gentlemen," shouted the Heavy Hardy figure, "It's only ten minutes to kick off so may I ask you to get ready to move into the hall."

"Do you suppose that's Edwin?" said Sylvia.

"No idea," said Bill, "but he has the air of a front row forward so he'd be a good match for Prunella."

Another five minutes went by and there was still no sign of the bride and her family. Just before four the registrar appeared and indicated to Heavy Hardy that the guests could now come in. This occasioned another announcement. "Ladies and Gentleman, would you please make your way into the building. We seem to be lacking the bride at present but Edwin's nipped off to give her a call. I just hope we don't have to bring someone in off the bench."

There was a nervous giggle from the crowd.

"Ah," said Harry, "so it's Little Laurel who's Edwin."

We all trooped into the building and found our seats. The minutes ticked by and the Registrar was clearly getting a little irritated. At quarter past four he pushed through the crowd and there was a muttered exchange between him, Edwin and Heavy Hardy. At that moment there was a flurry at the door and Prunella, wearing what at first sight seemed like a large pink bell tent, burst through, closely followed by Philip and Samantha.

"At last," said the Registrar, not bothering to be tactful. "Can we please get on with it?"

Edwin and Heavy Hardy made their way down to the front but, in spite of being urged forward by her father, Prunella didn't move.

"This is the wrong room," she said.

A collective sigh ran through the guests. The Registrar took a long deep breath.

"I assure you this is the correct room," he said.

"The room I booked was a bigger one."

"There is a bigger one but this is the one you booked. Now do you want to go ahead with this wedding, or don't you?"

"This is not the room I booked. I demand that we move to the other one."

That was clearly the last straw. The Registrar said very firmly. "Madam, you are already twenty minutes late. We do not have time to move to another room. In fact we no longer have time to conduct this wedding today. I must ask you all to leave and you will have to book another date." And with that he strode out of the room.

We all tumbled out into the car park again, wondering how much scotch Philip would need to get over this latest disaster. Before we could go looking for him, Heavy Hardy had yet another announcement to make. "Ladies and Gentlemen, I'm sorry for the confusion in there. Most unfortunate. We'll get it sorted, but in the meantime Prunella and Edwin have asked me to say that we may not have had the wedding but we can still have the reception so will you please make your way to the Community Hall on Primrose Street and we'll see you all there."

As the crowd began to disperse we spotted Philip and cornered him, keen to know what was really going on.

"Prunella had a few last minute nerves, did she?"

He looked at us in amazement. "Nerves? Prunella? You've got to be joking."

"So what happened to make you miss the off?"

Philip sighed. "Well, you see, a couple of weeks ago Samantha decided she wanted to sell her car."

By now we were getting used to the way Philip's stories always started at a tangent so we settled back to listen.

"She'd put an advert in the local paper but only a couple of people came to see it and they offered her well below her asking price. Then this afternoon, just as we're getting ready to leave, this guy knocks on the door unannounced and says he's come to look at the car."

"Bad timing," said Sylvia.

"You'd think so, wouldn't you," said Philip, "but Samantha had other ideas. She welcomed him in and took him straight out to see the car. I don't think her heart's really in this wedding," he added mournfully.

As we made our way towards the Community Hall Philip stayed with us. There was obviously something else he wanted to say.

"Look, I really appreciate you four coming to support me like this but there's something I forgot to mention. You won't know this, not having received formal invitations as it were, but the reception is, well, what can I say…."

"We're not invited perhaps," said Harry, cutting to the chase.

Philip looked horrified. "Oh, no, not that. Of course you're invited but …" He tailed off.

Sylvia caught my eye and mouthed silently. "Should have brought our own sandwiches."

"The thing is," said Philip struggling on, "well, these wedding plans have been, um … sort of chaotic from the beginning."

We all nodded. We had no problem with 'chaotic'.

"And when Prunella realised I was serious about

the fixed budget job, you know." We all nodded again. "Well, then she got all righteous and waste-of-money-ish."

I tried not to giggle as Sylvia mouthed: "Should have brought our own booze too."

"So the upshot of all this is", said Philip, "that it's a bit of a DIY reception."

"Meaning what, exactly?" asked Bill.

"Well, she's apparently organised the main meal – I don't know what it is – but I do know it's a bit basic. Also, round two is cheese and biscuits but the invites said 'cheese provided, bring your own biscuits and chutney'. And before you say anything, you're not to worry. I've brought biscuits and chutney for all of us."

There was a short silence as the four of us considered the extended implications of friendship.

"I think I need a drink," said Bill.

Philip looked embarrassed. "Ah, well …" he began.

"Don't tell me," said Harry, "pay bar. Yes?"

"Well, yes, but not to worry. I'll take care of you guys."

The event was definitely one of those occasions which began with very low expectations which were clearly not going to be achieved.

The Community Hall where the reception was

held had the air of a Scout Hut on its night off. The main meal turned out to be burgers and chips, the Chicken à la King having presumably fallen a victim to economy.

The bar was, well, perhaps limited is the best word unless you were very keen on cans of supermarket beer or sweet white wine. We bypassed the burgers, filled the immediate hunger gap with cheese and a couple of canned beers, and began discussing which pub we might head for to get a decent meal, when suddenly Philip pushed his way through the crowd towards us.

"Have you see Prunella anywhere?" he asked.

We looked a bit nonplussed. Losing the bride, even at a pseudo wedding reception, seemed more than a little careless.

"She and Edwin arrived together," Philip went on, but now we can't find her."

Suddenly there was a cry of anguish and we turned to see Edwin at the door, brandishing a piece of paper and yelling, "She's left me. She's run off with Jason."

Jason, we gathered out of the confusion, was the Heavy Hardy bloke.

"She left a note for me with the barman." He waved a piece of paper at us and Philip took it out of his hand.

"Sorry, Eddie," he read, "all I wanted was a wedding that was different. Jason says he knows a highland glen in Scotland where we can be married in a gypsy caravan."

"Oh, dear God," muttered Sylvia, "it's bloody Brigadoon."

As we slunk away to the nearest pub leaving Philip and Edwin to contemplate an away fixture rather than a home game, the final word of the day went to Samantha with an extremely non-maternal comment.

"Let's look on the bright side. At least if they're going to Scotland it will give us a chance to change the locks."

THE GREAT CAULIFLOWER CONFLICT

In terms of the world stage nothing much ever happens in my Village in the Valley but although it may seem a placid place there are many undercurrents just below the surface and periodically, like a rumbling volcano, these will erupt. One of the main flash points is our annual Village Garden Show. If it were possible to harness the power of the emotions and conflicting viewpoints at this event and feed them into the national grid, then there would be no need for wind farms.

Rivalries are inevitable in any village of course, but the annual Garden Show struggle between Ronald Trigg and Emery Jacobs was legendary. Some say it went back generations when their respective great-great grandfathers courted the same girl though the story doesn't say which one, if indeed either of them, won her.

But before we get to the tale of the Great Cauliflower Conflict, we must go back several months to the time when Granfer Butterball finally died. Granfer Butterball was Ronald Trigg's father-in-law and he had made it to 99 before finally choking to death on a fish bone in his throat while eating a smoked mackerel sandwich. He was mourned by all his family, not the least his daughter, Valerie Trigg, neé Butterball. None of us doubted that her sadness at her father's passing was genuine but we did feel it was also partly influenced by the fact that he was only a month off his centenary and the hall and catering for his party had already been booked.

In the event Valerie and Ronald did the sensible thing. The arrangements could not be cancelled so they decided to go ahead with the party anyway but call it a wake. However, that wasn't the end of it. To everyone's surprise, Valerie announced that her father had always wanted a green burial and that she'd made arrangements to have him interred in a field belonging to Morris Temple. Morris was a second cousin of her aunt's brother, which made the field a family field and, as it was also adjacent to the allotment where her father had spent so much of his time, it seemed an ideal place.

A green burial was a novel idea to many of us and inevitably our vicar, the Reverend Victor Coggles, objected as he does to most things that make any kind of sense. Equally inevitably our curate, Bev the Rev, thought it was a lovely idea and offered to conduct the service.

The Coggles reaction came as no surprise. Many of us struggle to understand how any institution can flourish in the 21st century with all the prejudices of the 16th, but Bev the Rev had not been with us long before we all realised that she was that rare thing in the clergy, a curate who thought of people before the system.

So, although Rev. Coggles humphed and ha-ed and "suggested" very strongly to Bev the Rev that she should have nothing to do with this "blasphemy", as he put it, arrangements for the green burial went ahead. It took a while as the paperwork required seemed endless but at last everything was arranged, people were invited, Valerie worked out an order of service, Morris brought his harmonica to accompany the hymns, arrangements were made for drinks in The Spy afterwards, the Reverend Coggles was told the wrong date to make sure he didn't turn up and then finally Granfer Butterball was laid to rest in a fenced off corner of Morris Temple's field which sloped down towards the village allotments.

"I thought that was very nice," said Valerie, drink in hand, as she thanked everyone for coming. "Now Dad can lie for eternity looking out over the vegetable patch he loved so much."

"And I'll be looking after it for him," said Ronald,

"keep him happy up in heaven like."

"Keep him laughing up in heaven if you're going to grow carrots up there, Ronald Trigg," said Emery Jacobs. "Right weird shapes, your carrots are. Reckon they must be cursed or something."

"It ain't my carrots what are cursed," yelled Ronald, "your carrots be so small, Emery Jacobs, that if they were green you'd think they were peas."

"My carrots be no smaller than them of yours," shouted Emery angrily, but at this point Dan stepped in and put a stop to the familiar argument.

"Now then," he said, "I'll have no carrot conflict in my bar. Specially not at a funeral. If you want to continue arguing you can go outside to do it." He glanced out the window. "And it's just started raining," he added thoughtfully.

Several months passed and then came the time for the annual Village Garden Show. This is a very different event from the village fete which is all about entertainment. The Garden Show, ostensibly a competitive display organised by the Village Hall Committee, is actually a battleground. It is held in a marquee erected on one of Roger's fields next to the river and it includes flowers, fruit and vegetables with various classes for different entries and different ages. The only group that is normally free of conflict is the *"Vegetables Grown by the Under-10s"* category, though even that was distinguished one year when Lisa Golding and Coriander Sanderson both claimed first prize due to the judge, an elderly short-sighted lady gardening writer, reading out a combination of their two names by mistake. That incident ended when Lisa rammed Coriander's Barbie doll into her prize marrow, while Coriander was doing her best to jam Lisa's shallots up their owner's nose.

That was unusual, but conflict amongst the adult contestants is the norm rather than the exception. Mostly, it takes the form of barbed comments and a re-arrangement of who sits next to whom in The Spy for the next few weeks, until memories fade and life gets back to normal – whatever that is in my Village in the Valley.

However, on this particular occasion matters were not resolved quite so easily. As mentioned before Emery Jacobs and Ronald Trigg were fierce competitors in the various vegetable classes, or at least some of them. Carrots were a case in point, other areas where they came head to head were onions, courgettes, and potatoes. However, there were certain vegetables where they had never clashed. Emery, for some reason, never grew broccoli and Ronald never grew cauliflowers and so when it came to these specific classes, peace reigned between them.

This year the first hint of trouble came as the

various contestants were bringing in their produce for display. Most people wanted to see what others had produced so there were many surreptitious glances as the various exhibits were placed and labelled. As usual Emery and Ronald were particularly keen to see how the other had done. This year, as so often before, Ronald's carrots were obviously superior to Emery's, but Emery's onions dwarfed Ronald's by a long way. Nothing unusual here, the two exchanged their usual insults about the others perceived failures but they both knew that what one of them gained on the swings, the other would gain on the roundabouts.

That is until Ronald brought in his final case which, when opened, revealed a wonderful display of cauliflowers. This stopped Emery in his tracks.

"What be they?" he demanded.

Ronald feigned puzzlement. "Well, they bain't be fish and chips, be they?" he said disingenuously.

"They be caulies," said Emery accusingly.

"Well done," said Ronald, "been reading a gardening magazine, have you?"

"You don't grow caulies," said Emery.

"Nothing in the rules to say I can't grow caulies if I want to."

"But you never have. You grow broccoli, I grow caulies and we fight over the rest."

"No reason I can't grow caulies," repeated Ronald

stubbornly.

"But you never have," was the best Emery could manage but Ronald just snorted and turned away.

Emery was clearly upset but even so it might all have ended there except Vera Witheridge had to put her oar in. I've noticed before that every village, every community always has at least one person who can be guaranteed to cause trouble at any opportunity. In My Village in the Valley it was Vera Witheridge.

Now she walked along the line of vegetables, sniffing as she went. She paused opposite Emery's exhibits, moved on to look at Ronald's, then came back to Emery's.

"Don't think much of them," she said, pointing at Emery's caulies. "Tiddly little things, if you ask me."

Behind her back, Ronald was grinning like the Cheshire Cat but we could all see that Emery was boiling.

"Think you must be losing your knack, Emery Jacobs," Vera went on with all the tact of a stripper in a WI meeting, "perhaps you ought to try and get one of those allotments up by Morris Temple's field as well."

At the time it just seemed like another of Vera's thoughtless and unkind remarks but in the light of later events we all wondered if she was being deliberately provocative.

And so we progressed to the judging. This year the Garden Show committee had persuaded Rufus Dingle to come and judge the exhibits. Rufus was a panel member of some gardening programme on the radio and it was considered quite a coup to have persuaded him to come to our little show.

He took the flowers first and all passed off fairly quietly. The expected entries came first, second or third and although there was some muttering amongst those who didn't win there was no major upset. The fruit judging went off in much the same fashion with only one small incident to mark it out from previous years.

This year Maureen Spurrier had entered a set of oranges. This was a new category as the rules stated the fruit had to be grown in the village and English villages aren't noted for their orange groves. However, a few years ago Maureen's daughter had brought some orange seeds back from Spain and without any serious intent Maureen had planted them in a pot in her conservatory. The resulting tree was quite pleasant but there had been no fruit until this year when suddenly, for no apparent reason, the tree produced six beautiful round, firm oranges.

Not surprisingly Maureen won that category as she was the only entry but the circumstances caused much amusement and encouraged Rufus Dingle to make a rather weak joke about global warming.

This meant there was a general attitude of relaxation when the vegetable judging began. It was not to last. At first everything went well. Emery won a first for his onions and Ronald won a first for his carrots. Humphrey Snape won a first for his potatoes with Ronald coming second, Harry won first prize for his broad beans with Emery coming second. Emery won another first for his leeks and Ronald another first for his radishes. So far, so good, everything normal. But then came trouble.

Ronald took first prize for his broccoli with Old Tomkins in second place. As usual Emery hadn't grown any broccoli. Then came the cauliflowers, normally Emery's chance to shine.

Almost as though he knew this category was going to be a bone of contention Rufus took a long time examining all the cauliflowers on display and finally made his choice.

"There is no doubt in my mind," he declared in ringing tones, "that these cauliflowers are amongst the finest I have ever seen. They may not be the biggest but in spite of what the ladies may tell you," he giggled lasciviously, "size isn't everything. These caulies are firm and have really excellent tight white heads. I have no hesitation in awarding first prize for cauliflowers to …" He paused to peer at the card on the table, "… Ronald Trigg."

There was uproar in the tent. Ronald was punching the air and yelling "Yes", Emery was yelling "No" and the rest of us who knew the history of their vegetable competitiveness joined in the general uproar.

Rufus Dingle just stood there, mouth open, looking like a man who thought he was on a litter pick and had just set off a land mine.

Eventually Hugo Framlington, the Village Hall chairman, managed to calm things down but as we all dispersed at the end of that Saturday afternoon I think we all sensed that this incident was far from over.

Both Emery and Ronald were amongst the crowd in The Spy that night but with some judicious manoeuvring that would have made a sheep dog proud, we managed to keep them well apart.

Rufus Dingle was there as well, holding forth about his broadcasting career and gardening in equal measure. He was staying overnight with Hugo Framlington so he could open the second day of the show on Sunday, the day when the all the produce entered was auctioned for charity.

He was leaning on the bar, pint of bitter in one hand, holding forth about competitions he had judged in a voice so loud that we wondered why his radio station needed a transmitter when all they had to do was to open a window. Hugo was smiling the smile that only a bored host can produce and no doubt thinking of The Times crossword puzzle awaiting him at home. Others were feigning attention while actually carrying on with their own conversation.

I'd long since tuned him out since I found the man and his subject totally boring, but suddenly Rufus banged his glass down rather hard and in the split second of silence following this, we heard him say: "Damn fine, caulies, those that won this afternoon. Don't know where they were grown but there must have been a good supply of nitrates in that soil and some very special compost, I shouldn't wonder."

No-one paid much attention at the time and the gentle roar of the crowd returned but I will always believe it was that remark that launched the final battle in the Cauliflower Conflict.

This took place the next day at around 11 o'clock. Tradition has it that the Chairman of the Village Hall Committee is the one who opens the marquee on the second day but on this occasion Hugo was late arriving, probably having been trapped over the toast and marmalade by Rufus Dingle. By the time he arrived a crowd had gathered, eager to try for some fruit and veg bargains while consoling themselves that it was all in a good cause.

Hugo came bustling up, Rufus Dingle strolling

behind. "Sorry, I'm late, sorry, I'm late," he squeaked and with a flamboyant gesture flung back the flaps to the marquee. We all poured in behind him and then came to a sudden halt. There, hanging from the roof right above the vegetable stand was a large sheet and on it was painted the words:

These caulies are not fit for human consumption. They was grown using human bodies as manure. No respect – not safe.

There was a silence, then with a roar of rage Ronald leapt across the tent and dragged the sheet down. "Tis all lies," he bellowed, "there's nothing wrong with my caulies. He's just a bad loser." And he pointed at Emery who was shouldering his way through the crowd.

"T'ain't lies," yelled Emery, "he wanted nitrates, he wanted special compost, that's why his missus's dad was buried up there in that field, to feed his bloody caulies, that's why."

This brought Valerie into the fray. "How dare you," she screamed, "it were my dad wanted to be buried in that field, nothing to do with caulies."

"Didn't do them no harm, though," yelled Emery.

At this point Rufus, characteristically, made the situation worse. "Am I to understand," he said, "that those prize-winning cauliflowers were grown in a cemetery?"

"Yes," said Emery.

"No," said Ronald and Valerie.

"I think we need to go somewhere else and have a quiet discussion," said Hugo but it was too late. Emery charged the vegetable stand and, grabbing hold of the cauliflowers started hurling them at Ronald. Ronald, I suspect more in self-defence than retaliation, grabbed the nearest missiles to hand and started hurling them back at Emery. The fact that it was Emery's onions he grabbed did nothing to defuse the situation. Within minutes everyone was at it, many of the other vegetable growers, initially anxious to protect their own produce but soon finding that defence was not enough, joined in and soon onions, plums, radishes, leaks, potatoes and – sadly – Maureen Spurrier's oranges were hurtling around the marquee.

Some of us waded in to try and restore order but it was a losing battle. The struggling crowd, many of whom were now spattered with fruit and vegetables of all kinds, surged out of the tent and across the field towards the river.

Suddenly the shouting and screaming was drowned out by the sonorous sound of 'Big Betty', the affectionate name of the largest bass bell in the church, ringing out across the meadow. Bev the Rev, quick on the ball as ever, had grabbed hold of Hubert, the bell captain and sent him scampering over to the church to ring the bell. The loud, ponderous tolling brought everything on the meadow to a halt. It was quite a picture – a crowd of people who a moment ago had been roaring their heads off now frozen in a shamefaced tableau, a marquee sagging on its guy ropes, fruit and vegetable debris everywhere, all halted under the rhythmic tolling of 'Big Betty'.

As the tension drained away Hugo Framlington suddenly said: "What happened to Rufus Dingle?"

We all looked round just in time to see Rufus, trying to clamber up out of the river, streaming water and covered in weed. In a moment the mood changed. A howl of laughter swept round the field even as some of us hurried forward to help him out. I'm sure I saw Hugo stifle a grin as he swept forward to offer apologies. To me it seemed a logical end to the great Cauliflower Conflict. I have long since ceased to be surprised at how often incidents like this in my Village in the Valley end up with someone in the river.

I don't know what the Village Hall Committee said to Rufus or what Rufus said to the Committee, but I strongly suspect they'll have to look elsewhere for a judge next year.

What will happen to the competition itself remains to be seen but I have heard that Emery has been making enquiries about broccoli plants and had got his daughter-in-law to go online for guidance on how to grow them. I fear there will be no neutral zones in next year's Village Garden Show but what Emery plans to use for compost, only time will tell.

WHERE DID THEY ALL COME FROM?

.

My Village in the Valley is a place where some people say the word 'normal' has been redefined but, of course, 'normal' is what you're used to. For example, no-one round here raises an eyebrow at such things as the notice at the end of Norah Fleming's farm lane which reads 'Bed and Breakfast and Butchers', though it has caused many an American visitor to develop a nervous twitch.

I don't think our village is especially different. It's small, of course, which perhaps gives it a more focussed identity but people are people wherever they live. Maybe it's just that when you know most of your neighbours by sight, if not always by name, then individual quirks of behaviour don't seem that strange.

Take Nan Mildew for example. In many ways Nan is totally conventional. She refuses to use the village shop on the Sabbath, she does her washing on a Monday morning and won't have anything to do with computers or "that internetty thing."

Well, she's not alone there. Many of our older inhabitants don't use computers but then most of them don't wear the sort of hats Nan wears either. She has a vast collection of hats, all different, all somewhat flamboyant in a wide variety of clashing colours. You can see her coming a mile off which can be quite useful if you can't spare half an hour to have your ear bent. A kind of headgear early warning system.

Nan's other little peculiarity is that she uses 'owls' as a unit of measurement. "That wall is three owls high," she'll say, or "my garden path is fifteen owls long which is a fair old distance to go and get the washing when it rains." By long experience we've worked out that there seem to be roughly two 'owls' to the yard but the history of this unconventional measure is completely unknown.

Then there's the matter of the village bike. This has been going on for so long so that most of us don't give it a second thought but for newcomers it is sometimes a concept too far. The origin of the bike is lost in the midst of time but presumably at some stage it did actually belong to one person. It is a perfectly ordinary bike, nothing fancy, black frame, straight handlebars, 3-speed hub gear. Not a bike with ambitions to compete in the Tour de France.

Theory has it that it was stolen from its original owner or, given the nature of village life, probably innocently borrowed with no actual intention of keeping it. However, it was never returned and ever since has simply passed from hand to hand (or foot to foot) as the need arose.

These days its most common resting place is outside the pub but it is equally likely to turn up leaning against someone's front wall, or outside the village shop or propped against the hedge in the churchyard. Somewhere along the line, it acquired a wicker basket on the handlebars and the unwritten convention is that if you come across the bike and there's something in the basket, that means someone is currently using it and you leave it alone. However, if the basket is empty then the bike is up for grabs, and if you need to get home in a hurry then you can take it and go, leaving it by your front gate for the next needy person to pass by.

In some ways you could say it is pure communism in action.

Most people in the village accept things like this as normal but occasionally you get incomers, who struggle to understand our way of life or simply don't want to know. Sholto and Lana Frobisher are a case in point. Rumour has it that they came from one of those high-rise tower blocks in south London but they weren't very communicative about their past so rumour it remained. Be that as it may, they bought Daffodil Cottage up the hill behind the main street. Now the cottages up there aren't large but they do have good sized gardens, dating from the days when the farmworkers who lived in them automatically grew their own vegetables to feed their families.

According to Harry, who always seems to know everyone, the estate agent who first showed the Frobishers round said they were very excited at the size of the garden and the fact that the cottage was so small that there wasn't room to swing a cat didn't bother them.

The Frobishers did have a cat, as it happens, or at least they did to start with. The cat, with remarkable astuteness, didn't wait around to test the swinging theory but decamped down the lane to Mrs Pettigrew's, only returning often enough to claim its territory and persuade Sholto and Lana that they were still responsible for the vet's bills.

When Sholto and Lana first arrived, the usual friendly overtures were made but while the newcomers were not rude, they were not welcoming either and we soon learned they preferred to keep themselves to themselves. What little knowledge we had of them came from seeing what they did in their garden.

The first thing they did was build some large

raised vegetable beds. Well, perhaps 'build' isn't quite the word, as they simply consisted of a number of planks held in place by bricks. The next thing was a lot of sawing and hammering and suddenly a large part of the garden was filled with what looked like hutches. In fact they were hutches and before long a lot of rabbits arrived and were installed. These were closely followed by a flock of chickens.

Chickens in the garden are commonplace round here but clearly the Frobishers did not understand the fundamentals of chicken behaviour as they installed 4 chickens and 4 cockerels and put them all in the rather small run together. Clara Evans who lives in the cottage next door to the Frobishers, tried to point out that this wasn't a very good idea but Lana was having none of it.

"One male for a group of females?" she said, "That's outrageous and immoral. Each chicken should have its own partner."

Clara tried to explain that chickens don't think in terms of morality but her advice fell on deaf ears so the chicken society experiment went ahead. It didn't last long, of course. In a short space of time there were three dead cockerels and one very battered and bleeding survivor. As Sholto and Lana had begun to look rather careworn at the constant 'cock-a-doodle-do' multiplied by four, a tactful silence was maintained and the three dead cockerels were not replaced.

It was fast becoming clear to their neighbours that Sholto and Lana had moved to the country to fulfil their own concept of a self-sufficient good life but without any real practical experience or knowledge to back it up.

Their vegetables were not a success. As far as observers could tell, their concept of vegetable gardening was to shove the various seeds into the soil and then leave them to get on with it. Weeding, watering, nurturing of any kind was clearly not understood or simply ignored. In spite of this some of the plants did battle their way to the surface and hopefully put out some leaves. Much good did it do them.

Which brings us to the rabbits. Sholto had built the hutches himself but, whatever other skills he might have possessed, carpentry was not one of them. The rabbits were constantly escaping and once out they demolished the few plants that had struggled through the neglect. Problem was they didn't stop with Sholto and Lana's plants, they quickly moved next door and continued the work of destruction amongst the neighbours until they were eventually rounded up and re-housed.

Mr Osbaldiston, who lives in the cottage on the other side of the Frobishers, was particularly upset when he discovered his carefully tended carrots, cabbage and cauliflowers shredded before he could harvest them. He went next door to complain but got short shrift.

"Rabbits will be rabbits," he was told, "and rabbits have to eat like the rest of us."

"They don't have to eat my caulies," retorted Mr Osbaldiston but all he got was a sad smile from Lana.

"We have to share our world with Nature," she said.

"No problem with that," said Mr Osbaldiston, "but when it comes to rabbits we've got enough wild ones out there already. What d'you want to go importing them for?"

The reply he got stunned him and caused many of us to blink when it was recounted to us later.

"We have to have lots of rabbits," explained Lana, "so we can breed them for meat."

"Meat?" said Mr Osbaldiston, "what's wrong with the butchers in town?"

Lana seemed puzzled. "Well, yes, that would do for now," she said, "but it won't be there much longer, will it?"

"Won't it?" said a bewildered Mr Osbaldiston.

"Well, of course not. Once the war starts all shops will close down and we'll all have to be self-sufficient. We're getting ourselves ready in good time."

Mr Osbaldiston was now thoroughly confused. "War? What war?" he asked.

"We're due a war anytime now," said Sholto patiently. "If you work it out on a sliding mathematical scale, we always have a war at regular intervals and the current one is already overdue. That's why we've come here, so we can take care of ourselves when the balloon goes up."

"Balloon? Who's talking about balloons?"

"It stands to reason that this period of peace cannot last much longer. We've left it a bit late really but if I can just stop the rabbits escaping it should all be okay."

"We're also getting some guinea pigs soon," announced Lana proudly, "I've been told they're very good in a stew."

Mr Osbaldiston couldn't quite see how she could reconcile guinea pig stew with 'sharing our world with Nature', but he had the sense to realise he was getting nowhere fast, so he beat a tactical retreat. The rabbit incursions continued of course so he solved the problem in his own way. He cleaned his shotgun and sat in his upstairs window. Every time he saw a rabbit in his garden, he shot it and as he was a very good shot, the rabbit population next door started diminishing rapidly.

Sholto and Lana were very upset, especially as

Mr Osbaldiston refused to return the dead rabbits to them.

"How do I know they are yours?" he argued, "they were in my garden and were probably wild ones."

"They can't be wild ones," protested Sholto, "our rabbits are disappearing."

"Not my problem," said Mr Osbaldiston and proceeded to add insult to injury by waiting until the wind was in the right direction then cooking a rabbit stew, the aroma of which floated over the fence into the Frobisher's garden.

This was in the days when Tom Riley was still our local policeman before the powers-that-be moved him away because he insisted on booking rich people as well as ordinary folk for speeding. Tom had lived in this area for years and believed in preventing trouble before it happened so he went to see the Frobishers, made soothing noises but pointed out that Mr Osbaldiston was within his rights to protect his own crops. Then he went next door and had a quite word with Mr Osbaldiston and suggested that perhaps the point had been made and maybe the shotgun should be put away again.

Mr Osbaldiston nodded thoughtfully. Privately he agreed. He'd already had one near miss when one of the Labradors belonging to the Grant family had come within his line of fire and he didn't want to fall out with any of his other neighbours. Much better to retain the moral high ground so he erected a wire fence round his vegetables, dug well into the ground to prevent the rabbits digging, and sat back to see what would happen next.

What happened next was that Sholto appeared in their garden one morning clad in a vest and shorts and carrying a large spade. Choosing a spot about halfway down the garden he began digging. After a few days he had achieved a large, though shallow, hole which had no apparent purpose. By now Mr Osbaldiston was not on speaking terms with the Frobishers but Clara Evans popped her head over the fence to ask what was going on.

"I'm preparing the ground for our air raid shelter," Sholto said, "I just hope I haven't left it too late."

This remark quickly ran round the village and caused a lot of speculation. Did these two know something the rest of us didn't? Was there really a war in the offing or were they, as the popular view had it, simply bonkers.

Given the ineptitude of our current government and the world situation in general, the more pessimistic in the village would not dismiss the war option completely, but for most of us it seemed unlikely. We certainly could not see the need of an air raid shelter in a small rural village like ours but we all agreed the Frobishers could do what they liked in their own garden.

The shelter made slow progress as Sholto proved as inept at digging as he was at carpentry and vegetable growing but he stuck at it and soon there was a sizable hole in the ground. He stopped short of laying his own concrete floor and got Matt Cookham, one of our local odd job men, to come and do it for him. Matt got quite enthusiastic about the whole project and stayed on to lend a hand. That's probably the only reason it got finished.

And finished it was, a deep brick-lined hole with a concrete roof and a stout door. It showed above the garden as a low mound with a sloping path leading down to the entrance. The mound itself was not unsightly but the huge piles of excavated earth all around it were. Neither Mr Osbaldiston or Clara liked the look of it very much but there wasn't anything they could do, and it did give the rabbits something to dig in when they escaped.

The Frobishers were clearly odd, but not exceptionally odd for this part of the world so the air raid shelter at Daffodil Cottage was a nine-day wonder and we soon forgot all about it. Forgot about it, that is, until the night of the big storm.

Periodically in this part of the world the elements get together to show us what they're made of. This particular night was very violent, high winds, lashing rain all preceded by huge claps of thunder. You can't do much about the weather so when a big storm hits we simply huddle down, wait for it to pass and hope the roof doesn't leak.

The morning after this particular storm it was still wild but the rain had eased off to an occasional flurry. Towards the end of the morning Mr Osbaldiston looked out of his window and noticed to his surprise that the Frobisher's chickens were still locked in their hutch. That was unusual as Sholto usually let them out around seven when he got up.

Then Mr Osbaldiston noticed that the contours of the Frobisher's garden had changed. There was no sign of the dome of their air raid shelter and the piles of earth surrounding it seemed a lot flatter. He thought for a moment then, neighbourliness overcoming antagonism, he went round to the Frobisher's house. He ignored the front door – front doors are rarely used in the village – but rapped smartly on the back door. No answer. He tried the handle and it opened so he put his head in and called out. "Anybody there?"

Silence. Now he was starting to get concerned. The chickens, having heard activity, were being very vocal so he decided he ought to let them out but as he began to make his way down the garden he thought he could hear faint shouts. He paused, turned his hearing aid up to maximum and listened again. This time there was no doubt, there were definitely faint shouts coming from somewhere nearby. Then in a flash he understood. The Frobishers had gone down into their air raid shelter, the storm had hit, redistributed the piles of earth and now they were buried.

He started to dig a hole in the earth with his hands, realised the futility of that so pausing only to shout: "Hang on, I'll get help" he scampered back next door and picked up the phone.

It is typical of our village that he never thought of ringing the emergency services but instead called Dan at The Spy. Within minutes Dan was sending out texts right left and centre while Mr Osbaldston found his largest spade and headed back next door where he began digging frantically.

Within minutes there was a crowd of people there with him – Bill, Harry, Sylvia, Roger, Dan from the pub, Jasper from the shop, Old Crested, Bev the Rev, Ronald Trigg, Emery Jacobs – all shovelling away like mad.

Even so it was a good half hour before they managed to clear a path down to the door of the shelter. Once there they realised the design fault that had caused the problem. The shelter door opened outwards and once the earth had fallen across it there was no way it could be opened.

The Frobishers were helped out into the open air, scared and shaking. Bill commandeered their kitchen and starting producing industrial gallons of tea while Sylvia and Bev the Rev took Lana upstairs and helped her into the shower and clean clothes. Forgetting past animosity Mr Osbaldiston took Sholto next door and did the same for him.

Finally everyone gathered in the Frobisher's garden for a quick post mortem. The Frobishers were pathetically grateful but also a bit bemused.

"We heard the thunder and thought it was bombs," said Sholto, "So we went down into the shelter."

In view of their recent experience no-one commented on this, but the remark of the morning came from Lana. "We've always kept ourselves to ourselves," she said, "but today, well I simply don't know where you all came from. It's wonderful."

They were truly grateful and thereafter were much more friendly, though nothing else changed, of course. They still attempted to grow vegetables, the rabbits still escaped at regular intervals and they simply redesigned the door of the air raid shelter to open inwards so life went on as normal – or what passes for normal in my Village in the Valley.

Though, thankfully, the war has never materialised. At least not yet.

THE FINAL YAP
OF THE WALKING
HEARTHRUGS

It always seems very quiet in my Village in the Valley but in some ways life here is a like a swan – calm and placid on the surface with a lot of frantic activity underneath.

Old Falstaff, who has a quote for every occasion, puts it like this:

> "With this, we charged again: but, out, alas!
> We bodged again; as I have seen a swan
> With bootless labour swim against the tide
> And spend her strength with over-matching waves."

That'll be from Shakespeare no doubt though for the life of me I couldn't tell you from which play. However, I'm certain about the Shakespeare because, as I may have mentioned before, Old Falstaff quotes him endlessly on every occasion – hence his village nickname. Well, that and the fact that he's almost a permanent resident in The Spy, where he occupies the same high backed wooden chair beside the log fire every night from October to the end of March. Then from April to September he moves outside to the old settle by the front door. One of our village's tourist attractions you might say, this big bellied man pouring his beer in through a magnificent set of whiskers, his elderly fox terrier, Moonshine, lying at his feet.

On this particular April evening he was sitting by the door as usual as I approached the pub. Moonshine, hearing my step, lifted his head briefly, clearly found me wanting and went back to sleep.

"Evening, Falstaff," I said as I pushed open the door.

"Anon, anon, sir. I pray you remember the porter."

Over the years I've found the best response to Old Falstaff's various utterances is to smile, nod and say nothing so I carried on into the bar. It was quite early and only Harry and Sylvia were there shaking their heads over the latest edition of the Goebbels News bulletin. That's not its official name, of course. It's actually the newspaper printed and distributed by our County Council setting out all the wonderful things it has achieved. To an uninformed outsider it may be impressive but the reality is very different. "All mouth and no trousers," as Bill once put it.

The item causing interest on this occasion was a piece about how much money the Council had saved which had enabled them to hold the Council Tax at the same level as the previous year. Admirable achievement, you might think, but as usual with the Council, the weasel words hid the reality.

"Micky Mouse accounting," said Harry, "saw enough of that when I worked in the City."

"At least the dodgy bankers were only interested in personal gain," said Sylvia, "which is understandable, if not acceptable. These buggers are just so scared of losing power that they'll do anything to hang on to it."

Norah Fleming, who had popped in with a notice about the village hall jumble sale for Dan to pin up by the bar, disagreed.

"Well, I think it's great that they're not putting the tax up," she said, "it's high enough as it is."

"That's the point," said Harry, "it is high. We're not getting any reduction but we're getting less for our money."

"Perhaps they're just being efficient," said Norah.

"Smoke and mirrors," said Harry, "these so-called savings have been achieved by dumping many of the services they're meant to provide."

"But they're still savings, aren't they?" said Norah triumphantly as the pub door banged shut behind her.

"Well, in one way she has a point," said Sylvia, "I

guess a lot of people think that no tax increase is a result."

The door opened and Nigel and Jessica came in.

"Falstaff's on good form tonight," said Nigel, "we've just been treated to something about jogging on footpaths."

"Can't see Falstaff going jogging somehow," said Sylvia.

Jessica gave the deep sigh she always uses when faced with our collective literary ignorance. "The actual quote is …

'Jog on, jog on, the footpath way,
And merrily hent the stile-a.'"

"Hent? What the hell is 'hent', asked Nigel.

"It means 'to seize' or 'to grasp'" said Jessica. It's an old English word that's obsolete now."

"Bit like our footpaths," said Harry. "In fact they're a good example of what we were talking about."

"What were we talking about?" asked Nigel.

"Theoretical council savings," said Sylvia.

"Ah, that again."

"Yes, that again," said Harry. "I can't understand why more people don't realise how they're being conned. Footpaths are a good example. The County Council is meant to keep all public footpaths clear but this is one of the things they've 'devolved to the local community', as they put it. Fair enough, I suppose if they also gave us the money to have it done but they don't. They achieve a theoretical saving on their budget and the Parish Council is left with the choice of finding enough volunteers to clear the paths or letting vegetation take over so they can't be used."

Although we didn't disagree, we know better than to let Harry get into full flood so I bought another round of drinks, we handed Goebbels News back to Dan so he could put it to better use in his cat's litter tray and Sylvia regaled us with the story of her aunt's parrot and the Jehovah's Witness.

It is said that things often come in threes and number two about local councils popped up the next day in the village shop. I'd gone in to buy my paper and found Jasper, who runs the shop with his wife Phoebe, having an animated conversation with Bev the Rev. Well, I suppose 'conversation' is misleading as that implies two-way communication. Jasper had Bev pinned back against the magazine rack and was giving her both barrels.

"You're not going to believe this," he was saying, "have you heard what they've done up at Holly Road School?"

Bev the Rev shook her head.

"They've only gone and cancelled playtimes there

'cos some people were complaining about the noise."

Jasper and his wife Phoebe have two young children at that school which is in the next but one village to ours so I had no doubt his information was correct.

Bev the Rev opened her mouth, but Jasper ploughed straight on.

"Lot of moaning minnies on that new housing estate reckon their peace and quiet is being disturbed by noisy kids in the playground. They've threatened to take out a noise abatement order against the school. What a load of cobblers."

I caught Bev the Rev's mute appealing glance and decided to intervene.

"That's nonsense," I said, "the school's been there for years and that housing estate was only built two or three years ago."

"That's right," said Jasper, "and it was always a bad idea, encircling a school with new houses. It was never going to work." He clutched my arm in his agitation. "We opposed that estate at the time. All us parents and a lot of the locals too. Too close to the school, we said, it would stop the school expanding and was always bound to cause problems."

"I remember," I said thoughtfully, "wasn't there a petition or something."

"There was," said Jasper, "signed by parents and

local residents. Something like eighty-five percent of local people objected but the planning authority just ignored them. And that's not all."

I caught Bev the Rev's eye and gave a little sigh.

"It's unbelievable," Jasper went on, "the school are so scared of legal action that they've banned all ball games in the vicinity of the school and they're also proposing to put up a sound-proof fence."

"That'll cost them a pretty penny."

"Yes, it will, and do you know how they're going to pay for it?"

"No...oo."

"They're going to use the money that was raised to buy school equipment, musical instruments and so on. When I think how many jumble sales and coffee mornings we held to raise that money, I could spit."

Bev the Rev took the opportunity to escape from the magazine rack. "Can't you appeal to your District Councillor?" she said.

Jasper snorted. "Him? He's a waste of space. Sooner he pops his clogs the better. The air he breathes could be put to much better use".

Bev the Rev looked rather taken aback at this but Jasper ploughed straight on.

"We tried involving him when the estate was first proposed but he supported it and on this issue he's already said it's unacceptable that local residents should have to suffer so much disturbance. So much disturbance I ask you." Jasper raised his eyebrows. "It's kids playing for God's sake, twenty minutes in the morning and fifteen minutes in the afternoon. Where's the disturbance in that?"

"Who is our District Councillor?" asked Bev the Rev.

"It's that twat, Kevin Tinker," said Jasper. "He actually lives in this village, would you believe. But when you need his help, he's never here."

"Kevin Tinker …? Oh, do you mean the man with the dogs?"

Jasper and I glanced at each other.

"Yes," said Jasper, "the man with the dogs."

At this point a word of explanation is probably called for. Kevin Tinker is, indeed, our democratically elected representative on the District Council. He was originally elected on a party ticket but after his second conviction for dangerous driving and various other offences the Council was rather coy about, his party disowned him and he is now technically an independent councillor. Though as Rupert once put it: "Incompetent councillor would be more accurate."

Unfortunately, he actually lives in our village, in one of the modern bungalows that were built behind the green. That was a contentious planning decision as well, but that's another story. I suppose

164

in fairness the man has to live somewhere but his presence among us is a constant reminder of his ineptitude though even that would be bearable if it wasn't for his dogs. He has three of them, all the same breed, whatever that is, all about four inches high, all looking as though they'd hit a wall at high speed and all with a snarl that is well out of proportion to their size. When Kevin takes them for a walk it looks for all the world as though he has three tiny hearthrugs on a bit of string, though Sylvia refers to them as 'rats on leads'.

Now we can't all be the same and if a man chooses to walk round the place dragging three snarling tacky looking hearthrugs behind him that's up to him. The problem lies in the noise they make. During the day it's merely irritating. Kevin gives them the run of his garden which is perfectly safe as I doubt they'd have the ability to jump over a matchbox, let alone a garden wall but it does mean that if they see – or sense – anyone within a hundred yards they embark (no pun intended) on a fusillade of furious yapping.

Now in a village like ours there are a lot of dogs and they're by no means silent. Hugo Framlington's spaniel has a strong objection to pigeons and lets them know it. Philip and Samantha Bracebridge have a greyhound who seems to resent postmen, vocally only fortunately. Jessica has a beagle who insists on issuing a challenge to every other dog it comes across and Doreen Fawcett has a Pyrenean Mountain dog, nearly as tall as she is, a friendly animal which greets everyone it meets with a low rumble that sounds like an impending earthquake.

Then there are the two golden retrievers belonging to Jasper and Phoebe. They're mostly very well behaved but don't like the sound of police or ambulance sirens. They hear them long before we do and they let out a long, echoing mournful wail that persists until the sound of the sirens have faded into the distance. That can be a bit disconcerting but it has the virtue of being short, as do all the other dog utterances in the village. They bark, snarl, woof or grunt in response to certain events or people and then they stop. Not so Kevin's dogs. Once the hearthrugs start yapping they can go on for an hour or more, which is extremely irritating.

However, it is much worse at night. We've never discovered what sets them off in the small hours – it certainly isn't sirens, which they ignore. They might go several nights in silence and then suddenly, for no apparent reason, they let rip around two in the morning, waking everyone within earshot. It doesn't help that they're small enough to get in and out of the house through the cat flap.

There have been complaints, of course, but they

fall on deaf ears. Kevin denies the dogs go out at night, denies that they make any noise and says that if they did he would hear it too and he doesn't. Whether he is lying or whether he is a very sound sleeper or whether he is so inured to their yapping that he no longer hears it, is a subject for conjecture. But the yapping goes on.

I remember one gathering in The Spy when what to do about the yapping hearthrugs was the topic of conversation. Muzzles were suggested but that would require Kevin's co-operation which was unlikely to happen. Dan suggested super-gluing the cat flap so at least they would stay in at nights. Jessica suggested trying to run them over but as they only went out of the garden when Kevin took them for a walk that might prove tricky.

"Don't see why," said Sylvia, "run him over too. Solve a lot of problems." Sylvia lives in a cottage that's well within earshot of the night yapping so she is hardly an impartial commentator.

Ronald Trigg offered to shoot them if we had a whip round for his fine and Bill came up with the idea of digging a pit in Kevin's garden then putting sharp stakes at the bottom, camouflaging the lot with twigs and grass. "Like they do in all the best jungle films," he said cheerily. We took this to be a joke, though with Bill, late of the Royal Engineers, you're never quite sure.

In the end the yapping hearthrug problem was solved in a way that could probably only have happened in the village like ours. It was April and, with the local council elections due in a few weeks, Kevin Tinker obviously decided he needed to do something positive. He appeared at the door of The Spy one evening dragging the yapping rats on leads behind him.

"Evening all," he said but before he could get any further Dan cut in. "You can't bring those …" he hesitated, "… dogs in here."

"Why not?"

"'Cos they're too noisy. If you want to come in, you leave them outside."

Kevin obviously didn't like this but he was determined to do his positive canvassing so he retreated and returned a few minutes later, hearthrug free.

"Now then," he said rubbing his hands together, "can I buy anyone a drink?"

There were no takers but he persevered. "Good to have a chance to chat," he said, "now are there any local issues that you think the Council should be dealing with?"

"How long have you got," muttered Harry but Sylvia was more direct.

"Noise abatement," she said, "Three small rats masquerading as dogs round the village green for a start."

Even Kevin, who had all the sensitivity of a squashed earwig, could not miss this reference.

"I've told you before," he said, "that my dogs do not make a noise. Just the occasional bit of gentle barking like any other animal."

"Hearthrugs don't normally bark," said Nigel.

"Neither do rats," said Sylvia.

"I do wish you wouldn't call them rats," said Kevin, "they're dogs. They may not be pedigree dogs, but they are unique."

A howl of laughter greeted this announcement and Kevin realised he was a hiding to nothing.

"Right. Time to go. I'll just say I hope you'll all vote for me next month. After all, I am the Councillor who Cares."

There was an even louder roar of laughter and Kevin turned on his heel and left the pub. A moment later we heard a scream of anguish. We rushed to the door and outside we found Kevin contemplating three dog leads, all chewed through and no sign of any dogs.

"My dogs," he cried, "what's happened to them?"

We all struggled, with various degrees of success, to look vaguely sympathetic.

Kevin looked round frantically and then his gaze fell on Old Falstaff sitting on his settle. "Oy, you," Kevin bellowed, "you were out here. Did you see what happened to them?"

Old Falstaff looked up from his beer. Moonshine lay in his usual state of slumber beside him.

"And Caesar's spirit, ranging for revenge,
With Ate by his side come hot from hell,
Shall in these confines with a monarch's voice
Cry "Havoc!" and let slip the dogs of war," he said.

Kevin looked baffled – as well he might – but then seized on the one word that seemed to make sense to him.

"Ate," he screamed, "are you telling me something ate my dogs?"

"Oh, for heaven's sake," said Jessica impatiently. "He's quoting Shakespeare. Those lines are from Julius Caesar and "Ate", with a capital A, was the goddess of ruin and strife. Don't be so literal. I don't know where your rats, sorry dogs, have gone but they have not been eaten."

She made her statement in all good faith but at that moment I happened to catch Old Falstaff's eye and he gave me a drooping wink, glancing down as he did so. I followed his gaze and saw Moonshine, apparently fast asleep as usual. From what I knew about fox terriers I suspected they thought hearthrugs were for sleeping on but rats would be another matter.

I kept my thoughts to myself. I didn't actually believe that Moonshine had eaten the dogs. Even if he had the capacity, he wouldn't have had the time. On the other hand, the broken leads had a decidedly chewed look about them so maybe Moonshine had just encouraged fate to take a hand.

Two weeks later Sylvia came into The Spy one evening waving a local paper from our nearby seaside town. We wondered why she thought we might be interested in '*Pier Re-opens After Seaweed Infection*' or '*Fight Breaks Out at Ludo Contest for the Over 80s*' but she brushed aside our questions, and pointed to a small advert on the back page.

It had been placed by the *Yippy Yappy Dog Rescue Centre* and showed a picture of three immaculately trimmed lapdogs with the caption "Could you give these neglected little darlings a home?"

"Do those look familiar?" she asked. We all peered at the photograph. Then we looked at each other and decided we didn't really want to know.

The week after that, at the local council elections, Kevin lost his seat and his deposit. We were never absolutely certain what happened to the yapping hearthrugs but as far as the village was concerned it was a happy ending all round.

ABOUT THE AUTHOR

Michael Bartlett has written for radio and television for over 40 years. He has been a regular writer for hit programmes such as *The Archers* (Radio 4), *Rainbow* (Thames TV) and *Jackanory* (BBC), and he has also written numerous original plays which have been staged for radio, TV and theatre across the UK.

He has worked as a Director in BBC Children's Television, producer in BBC Schools Radio and BBC Radio Drama, Programme Controller of a commercial radio station, and Production Director and editor for an audio production company.

Michael has also served as the Chairman of The Children's Film Unit, Chairman of Factotum Theatre Company and on the board of The Attic Theatre, Wimbledon.

He is a Life Member of The Writers' Guild of Great Britain.

Michael's books include short story collection *Personal Islands*, and memoir *Out of the Blue*.

He lives with his wife in Norfolk.